# Thune's Vision

A collection of stories

By Schuyler Hernstrom

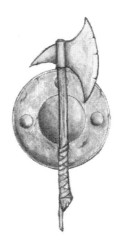

2016

First Printing: 2016

*The Challenger's Garland* copyright 2014, originally appeared in Heroic Fantasy Quarterly, Issue 20.

# Table of Contents

# The Challenger's Garland

Molok rose from his resting place in the damp earth. He mounted his black warhorse and rode through gray mist, past broken tombs and stunted trees. Before a cliff's edge he brought the mount to heel. Tendrils of fog coalesced in the heavy air, weaving themselves into a bridge of sorts, leading away into the void beyond the sky. Molok snapped the reins and crossed over, entering the realm of his lord.

At that moment the realm appeared as a quaint coastal scene. Under low clouds dunes dotted with patches of grass gave way to a wide beach. The King of Death chose as his form a graceful sea-elf. His lithe body sat relaxed against a derelict boat half buried in sand. Nimble fingers guided a netting needle through lengths of rough line. Beside him on the sands a large crab sat watching the effort. Molok dismounted and bent the knee. The sea-elf waved his hand impatiently.

"Rise."

Molok did as he was bade.

The sea-elf spoke again. "The dryads of Monnos imagine I collect souls in a giant net. I thought I would try my hand."

The King of Death raised the net for Molok's inspection. The Black Knight said nothing.

The crab at the sea-elf's feet spoke in a high voice, "Fine work, my lord."

The sea-elf nodded. "Thank you, Locken." He set the net down and reclined. His beautiful eyes, the color of sea foam, met the knight's red gaze. "Molok, The Black Knight, my most beloved servant. What brings you to my court?"

"I dreamt."

Locken made a chittering sound with his mottled blue claws.

The sea-elf spoke, "Indeed? The deep sleep of Death is a gift bestowed upon all my servants. To dream is irregular."

Molok's otherworldly voice carried over the sound of crashing waves. "I dreamt of a white citadel."

"A white citadel? Most interesting."

"A castle of white stone, atop tall cliffs where wyvern nest and the sea meets the land. On the drawbridge a champion in white armor chased in gold stood waiting."

Locken stroked his mandibles with a gnarled claw. "He speaks of the fortress of Azal, the seat of Triment, one of the kingdoms that still denies the inevitability of your rule, my lord."

"I believe you are correct, dear brother." The sea-elf stood to face Molok. "Well, Black Knight, I give you leave to seek out this fortress. Ride under my banner and wear the garland as champion and emissary. Slay the champion of Azal. Surely this is the meaning of your dream."

Molok went to his knee again. The King of Death bent to kiss the ornate black helm. The audience was concluded. The knight led his horse along the beach. Locken sidled next to him.

"Tell me, sir knight, how many champions have you slain?"

"I could not say. I sleep. I rise to lead my lord's armies. I slaughter all who oppose his will, as you know, trickster. I have never been defeated. The weeping of widows is my lullaby. The crows fat with the flesh of the slain are my companions."

"Your existence certainly lacks ambiguity. Do you recall nothing else?"

"What else should I recall?"

The crab playfully nipped at Molok's greaves. "Nothing, I suppose."

Molok traveled back over the bridge and took the western road. On his lance fluttered the banner of the King of Death. His steed's hooves made the sound of a heavy drum on the packed earth. The gray lands that bordered his lord's receded in the distance.

The road became treacherous as the shadows of the Murkem Mountains loomed. The stunted craftsmen of the snow capped peaks fled behind their thick gates at his approach. Onward he rode, black armor encrusted with frost.

At the base of the mountains stretched the vast Azarzi. The black steed traveled tirelessly over the wind swept dunes and past nameless ruins. The nomads gave him a wide berth, chanting their prayers into the starry night to ward off the ill omens that trailed in the wake of the black rider.

In the Kinnivesse jungle the apes scattered from his shadow, scurrying up the massive trees in which stood their wondrous city. They peered down from latticed towers, unwilling to shower the lone horseman with missiles, as was their usual practice. The towering trees shrank as the jungle ended.

9

He entered a land of rolling hills and verdant pasture.

Molok dismounted, walking through a field of flowers. The grass was still fresh with dew. Ahead he saw the silhouette of a young woman. She turned upon hearing his heavy steps. Her face was round and healthy.

"I hear the step of an armored knight. Are you from the citadel?"

Molok looked into her eyes, two orbs of milky white without iris or pupil.

"No, child. I am the knight that serves the King of Death."

The girl spoke sadly, "Then the armies of night have at last entered Azal."

"No. I ride as champion, alone. I seek flowers for a garland to obey the ancient convention."

Molok's red eyes watched as the girl deftly plucked wildflowers from their stems. She worked without haste, weaving the stalks skillfully into an artful ring.

"Kneel, then, Black Knight."

Upon his brow the blossoms withered. He mounted the warhorse and resumed his journey.

Lobon, Champion of Azal, woke from a dream. He lay a while, pondering the image of the black rider that haunted his sleep. For weeks the visions had come with increasing clarity. He could now remember glowing red eyes peering from the visor of the horned helm. The knight was mounted on an ebon destrier, wisps of smoke wafting from its nostrils. His wife, Mehvi, stirred.

"The dream again?"

"Yes."

Lobon rose and threw water on his face from a basin.

## The Challenger's Garland

Through the narrow window he saw the sun peeking over the horizon, bathing the green fields of Azal in red and purple light. Mehvi slipped her arms around his trim waist and laid her face on his back. Her lips grazed a long scar, one of many. Lobon sighed.

"I was young once, and felt immortal. I was swifter and stronger than any of Azal's foes. Now my temples are graying. Old wounds ache. And the black rider haunts my dreams."

"You speak nonsense. You have never been defeated and you never shall. Peace will come eventually and we will grow old together."

"To die in my sleep, racked with infirmity and unable to even recall the days when I stood as Azal's chosen, knee deep in the corpses of my foes."

Mehvi came to face him. "First you fear death in battle, then you fear to die of old age?"

Lobon snapped, "I fear nothing! It is a feeling I cannot describe. To face a man in combat, to cut him down, to watch the light dim as the soul slips its bonds, it is... I cannot put it into words. It is a heady wine. And I have been drunk for decades. To become sober, whether by death or retirement, I cannot imagine it. Now time catches up with this body and Azal's foes still march. And the black rider..."

Mehvi gently led him back to bed. A knock disturbed them. A retainer stood outside with a message.

Molok, servant of the King of Death, was riding through Azal bearing the flower garland of a challenger and flying his master's standard from his lance.

Lobon rose and began to prepare himself.

Molok sat mounted, awaiting the appearance of the

Champion of Azal. Before him the white citadel gleamed bright in the noon sun. Ahead on the road his garland lay, thrown to the ground in a ritual gesture. Petals from the desiccated blooms were carried aloft by a light wind. Spectators on ramparts cheered as Lobon rode over the drawbridge. He guided his white stallion to stand before Molok.

"Welcome to Azal, Black Knight. I am Lobon, the champion."

Molok nodded in response. Lobon's mount was agitated so close to the black warhorse. He worked the reins, bringing it under control. He studied the black knight. The warrior's ornate plate armor seemed ancient, the craft of centuries past. The helm was of an even older style. Wisps of floating ash slipped from places where the heavy plates joined. The red eyes stared straight at the white champion. Molok spoke, his voice resonating malice.

"A dream bade me come here. The Fates single you out for slaughter for reasons only they comprehend."

Lobon laughed. "I have never been defeated, fell servant."

"Nor have I."

"Tell me, black knight. Were you once a man or are you purely of night and woe, a creature of the King of Death's making?"

"It does not matter."

Lobon shrugged. "Indeed, it does not." The champion urged his mount back to the bridge. He saluted the black knight and both lowered lances. The steeds reacted swiftly to their masters' commands, thundering violently toward each other, nostrils flaring and eyes glazed with animal fear. At the last moment the white stallion reared, throwing Lobon to the ground as Molok's lance grazed the white champion's

12

shield. The stallion galloped off in terror. Lobon stood painfully, drawing his sword.

"Apologies. My mount could not find the courage."

Molok dismounted, drawing his axe from its sheath on his steed's flank. He advanced. Lobon gave ground, drawing the black knight off the road. Molok tested his foe with a series of tentative swings, letting the weight of the axe's broad head deliver much of the force. Lobon parried skillfully, moving his body to escape the force of the strikes and preserve his shield. When Molok sensed Lobon had established a rhythm the black knight rushed forward, slamming his shoulder into the shield and throwing Lobon off balance. The white champion twisted desperately to avoid the killing blow. The axe whistled through empty air. Lobon raised his sword high. Molok was the veteran of a 1000 duels. He knew he could not get his shield around in time. Instead he lunged forward. The two crashed together like metal bulls, grasping and heaving, desperate to gain leverage. Lobon lost his footing and the two stumbled, still locked in each other's arms.

The momentum carried them both rolling down the steep hill atop which the citadel sat. At the bottom the two stood. Molok's eyes glared as he rained blows upon Lobon's cracking shield. The champion countered, thrusting upwards, catching the edge of Molok's helm and sending him backwards. Molok howled, enraged.

The two traded blows, increasingly desperate, all attention to form lost. The duel ranged over a field of wheat and into a marsh. At a safe distance Locken watched, now in the guise of a red fox. Mud and fetid water slowed the pair, grasping their feet. Lobon's breath came in gasps. Molok's axe thundered down, finally shattering the champion's shield. Another blow rent the champion's pauldron and bit deep.

Warm blood coursed from the wound. With a yell Lobon closed the gap between the pair, grasping the black knight with his free hand and pushing him back. His arms felt leaden. His legs ached. Was this what his foes had felt before the killing blow fell? He tried to raise his sword but lost his balance and fell back into the muck. Molok raised his axe and came forward. Lobon lay his head back on a tussock of brown grass. Death was coming. He had heard men in similar circumstances, those that had miraculously survived, describe feelings of calm. But he felt only simmering anger.

"Tell me, Black Knight, I demand you tell me. Were you once a man? Grant me this knowledge at least."

Molok paused. He lowered the axe and stood, staring at an invisible horizon. He saw the blind girl's hands again, dexterous and alive. The black knight could vaguely recall the feeling of their flesh, warm and smooth. But he had not touched her, nor any others. The impressions floated like the notes of song distantly heard. More came, unmoored now from places deep within the mind. There was the warmth of the hearth. A child at his knee. The memories evaded capture.

During the reverie Lobon steeled himself, marshaling his waning strength. Molok returned to the present with a wail of mournful rage. The black knight brought the axe down with all his fell might. With great effort Lobon rolled away from the blow. The axe sunk deep into the mud. Molok tried desperately to free it, sinking himself even deeper. Lobon stood and raised his sword. The blade found the space between helm and gorget. The black knight's severed head fell into the muck. A keening wail grew as trails of Molok's black soul whipped free from the armor. Before Lobon's eyes the armor disintegrated and the soul stuff was drawn back

14

into the earth. Only the helm remained. Lobon collapsed, the loss of blood finally unknotting his soul from its earthly tether. Into the narrowing tunnel of his vision the fox appeared.

"Take the helm, champion, 'tis your destiny and your right. Hurry now! Before the ghost leaves you!"

Lobon whispered. "I have never been defeated."

"And never you shall! You are stronger than the last. Place the helm upon your head and glory in battle until the end of time!"

With difficulty Lobon sat up. He removed his helmet and took the black helm in his gauntleted hands, stained in blood and filth.

"Hurry!" Locken implored.

The helmet descended over his handsome face. The world fell away. His kingdom and family, the green land of Azal, the smell of baking bread and the taste of wine, the crisp autumn air the morning of the hunt, all were cast into black void. His white armor blackened, absorbing the shadows that hung heavy under the gnarled willows. His new eyes glowed red. He was a thing of anger and battle. He was proud. He would never be defeated. Suddenly at his side the black steed waited. He took the axe and mounted. The fox followed discretely behind, all the way to the gray lands.

# Athan and the Priestess

Athan's band reached their village as the sun dipped low in the mud gray sky. The warlord sat upright in his saddle, chin high, wind whipping his black curls against the furs around his shoulders. He was rightfully proud, having led his tribesmen in another successful raid. Two score of slaves, unworthy folk from the villages along the steppe's forested edge, would soon be added to the village's wealth.

Dark silks fluttered in the dusty breeze as the women rushed to greet the returning warriors. A wail went up here and there as a few learned they were now widows.

A thin hand pulled at Athan's cloak. The grim warrior looked down to see Ceki, the wizard's boy, staring with earnest expression.

"Lord Athan, come quickly! Thune is at death's door! He waited for you! He must speak with you!"

With a muttered curse Athan handed the reins to a nearby slave and followed the boy through the rough hewn wooden gate.

The candle's flame wavered as Athan pushed aside the tattered hide which served as door. A voice croaked from the gloom.

"Warlord, you have returned."

"Indeed. Speak your message quickly so that I may join my men in drink. Our raid was a success. Another verse added to the song of my name."

From the darkness came a derisive snort.

The warrior seated himself in the center of the tent. As his eyes became adjusted to the near darkness his host became visible, slumped atop a mound of filthy cushions. The earthy smell of mushrooms competed with the sharp aroma of incense in the close air. A silver dish dark with patina lay on the carpet, strewn with the stems of yudh, the sacred fungus which loosened the tether which held the soul inside its body.

The wizard's gaunt face affected an expression of utter disdain. "You should concern yourself with other matters, matters of greater import than carousing with your warriors. Someday you will die by blade or arrow, or grow old and weak. Your song of meaningless raids and duels will be forgotten."

"Speak your message, cursed one."

Thune struggled to rise, leaning forward finally with the help of his wives. In the oily light his eyes were black orbs, pupils swollen under the effects of the yudh. He spat once and began his tale.

"The gods of Change and Death bade me come to them in the other-world. I ate the yudh, again and again, until I could pierce the darkest part of the veil that separates this world from theirs. Past the Jade Gate I came upon a desolate land, windswept wastes watched by a towering pyramid of gleaming obsidian. Change and Death waited, swathed in white robes, heads hooded. I knelt before them and then under the swirling orange skies of that blasted land they gave me prophecy."

Thune lurched forward, heaving black bile onto the

matted furs of the hut's floor. His first wife wiped the mess from his face as he continued in a choking voice, extending a bony finger toward Athan.

"I saw you! They showed me your path! How the world may be rent and yet remade!"

"Ha! And what am I to do, wise one?"

"The wall above the river, the barrier that separates us from the Ullin, you must breach it. You must find the high priestess and become one with her. The scion of your union will sunder both lands and bring light and dark together again so that mankind is whole!"

Athan smiled his crooked smile and cocked his head.

"Why should I do that?"

Thune spat dark blood at the warrior's feet and hissed.

Gasping, he spoke, "Fool! Since long ago when the priests of the Ullin raised the barrier and stopped the war we have grown weaker every year, fighting amongst ourselves, killing and raiding. Someday we will be but animals, fighting for scraps of the mammoth carcasses that dot the steppe. The barrier must fall! The war must be resumed. The Ullin lands will be conquered and we may flourish again, mighty kings and queens, not petty warlords and raiders."

"It is a pretty vision. And no doubt false, as all the gods are liars. But even if I were to accept this quest the barrier is impassable. None of us may cross the river or land upon their coast. Thus the Ullin live in peace and safety."

"The kiss of the sea witch will permit you to breathe under the deepest water. See her and beg her favor. Then cross under the barrier, through the river, and seek the priestess in the land of the Ullin. Forget your pathetic songs of pathetic raids! Begin the dynasty that will make the world anew and lay waste to the arrogant Ullin!"

Athan scoffed. Thune crawled forward, grasping at the warrior's jerkin, thick leather embellished with scales of dark steel. His breath was hot and reeked of sick as he neared.

"You must! I have seen it!"

The warrior pushed at Thune but the wizard was granted the strength that comes under the shadow of imminent death. The wizard spoke again, a husky whisper, his cracked lips now mere inches from Athan's face.

"You are a coward! The gods have shown me the future and you reject your destiny!"

The warrior strained against the wizard's iron grip.

"I am no coward!"

"Then swear an oath!"

Athan made the oath as Thune breathed his last. The seer's eyes rolled back into his head as bile gurgled from his twisted mouth. His body convulsed and was still finally. The seer's wives wailed as Athan left, brow dark and mouth downturned.

His slaves knelt at the entrance to his hut. Yelk, the elder, reached up, handing his master a skin of mare's milk, fermented. The warlord drank deep. He threw the skin down and ordered Yelk to wake with the dawn and saddle his horse.

Yelk spoke, eyes never leaving the ground, "What bothers our master?"

Athan bristled at being addressed by a slave. But he permitted Yelk the familiarity; the man had served the warlord's family since before his birth.

"That foul Thune used his last breath to implore me undertake a strange quest."

"Our master will surely be successful."

Athan made a sound of derision. He unsheathed his blade and handed it to Yelk.

"See to the blood and oil it. Mind the gore caked around the hilt. And send someone to the slave pens and fetch one of the new women that bear my mark. Bring me the one with long hair and green eyes."

The warlord pushed aside the drape of hide and entered his hut. The sun sank into the horizon, sheathing the west in a warm glow.

He set off at dawn while the village still lay in a fugue from the night's excesses. He rode northwest, making for the coast. After a few hours ride the river, the Belt of the World as it was known, and its ethereal barrier became visible in the distance. From its banks rose shimmering bands of wavering blue light, the impenetrable wall which had brought an end to war and began the slow demise of the sorcerer kings of old, Athan's distant ancestors. They were haughty men who lived only to wage war upon the Ullin. To the south lay the steppe, crossed here and there by chasms where the earth had been rent in ages past by their powerful spells. Steam rose from the ancient wounds, carried away by the steppe's whipping winds.

A day's hard ride brought the warlord within sight of the line of jutting rocks where the sea witch made her home. Skulls on poles warned against his approach. Wisps of hair clinging to bare bone stirred in a wind heavy with salt. He made a small fire amidst the low dunes and ate a meal of cured meat. Sleep was long in coming. Underneath the distant sound of crashing waves the warlord imagined he heard a woman singing a song of mourning. The cry of gulls woke him after dawn.

He left his horse tethered to one of the grim signposts and made his way to the rocky beach. A pair of seaweed strewn steles rose before him as the ground sloped to meet the lapping water. Under their cloak of rotting green were scribed runes worn nearly smooth by the tides.

Athan stepped back with a start as he watched a woman rise from the water. Her skin was smooth and blue white, the pristine hue of the freshly drowned. Water flowed from the black hair which reached past her waist, locks interwoven with kelp and seashells, laying across her heavy hips and breast.

"Warrior, why have you come here? The smallest child in the poorest village knows this is my beach, knows I do not welcome visitors."

A tremor passed through Athan's muscular frame. Here before him was the other worldly beauty of a being born of gods, the bastard daughter of the god of the sea and the goddess of beauty. She was cursed to remain amidst the rocks until the end of time. It was her mother's curse, to keep the daughter's beauty far from the dark depths where her father dwelled in intermittent slumber.

Athan spoke, "I mean no offense. I desire your kiss, that I may cross under the barrier atop the Belt of the World and seek a destiny foretold by a seer."

The sea witch smiled and replied, "Well, you are a bold one." She paced slowly, walking around Athan, looking him up and down. She continued.

"Though malice lurks in your eyes I find you strong and well-favored. I am inclined to grant your request. But what should I ask in return?"

"I do not know."

Her black eyes looked down as she pondered. A smile

graced her bluish lips as inspiration struck. "But I do know, warrior. You will give me a child, someone to keep me company here. I have many children but none so witty as to amuse a daughter of gods."

"That is easy enough."

She smiled at his easy acquiesce. Her voice was pleasant to his ears, a birdsong laden with notes of an unfathomable divinity. Her plans became more elaborate as she thought aloud.

"I would bear twins. Like the first man and woman, and thus make my own race. I will love them and cherish them, so unlike my cruel mother and father."

She stepped forward. Athan felt his blood rising. Her eyes bored into him, black orbs wherein lay all the mysteries of the ocean. She spoke again, a hushed whisper, the mode of all lovers.

"A kiss then."

Her lips were cold against his. She took his hand and led him into the water. After a moments panic he realized he could breathe the same as he had on land. A battalion of creatures, eels, crabs, and other beasts of the sea swam about him as she led him deeper. Her servants removed his clothes and cast them ashore with his belt and weapons. Deeper they went, coming to walk on a field of large, smooth stones. She led him to a bed of swaying blue moss where they became lovers under the wavering beams of soft light that drifted down from the distant surface above. Her body grew warm underneath him as she writhed, moaning, a low sound that carried through the dense water to far places.

Afterwards Athan rested on the moss as the sea witch stood, moving languidly in the fading glow of pleasure. She stood and stretched, then began to spin slowly as she danced and sung to herself softly.

Dark shapes passed overhead. The warlord rose on his elbow, watching the silhouettes circle.

The sea witch paused to face Athan, smiling as she spoke, "Thank you, warrior. Your seed will grow strong in me. The blood of the sorcerer kings will mix with that of gods. And now you may serve another purpose. My old children, those you see above, the poor dear things must wait long for the opportunity to taste the hot blood of those that dwell on the surface. I could not deny them such a pleasure."

The shapes descended. Athan scrambled into a wide crevice, narrowly missed by a gaping maw lined with row after row of saw teeth. He looked to his right and left, desperate for some path to safety. His feet were suddenly beset with sharp pains. The floor of the crevice was alive with crawling things, things of shell and claw, grasping, piercing his naked flesh.

Yelling an oath he sent himself forward with a push of his strong legs. Two of the beasts descended immediately. In their haste they spoiled each other's aim, granting the warrior a short respite. The sea witch danced and sang her songs as her children flicked their tails in rage. Another of the long monsters dived toward him. Athan launched himself at the creature, twisting to avoid the terrible mouth, grabbing its dorsal fin as it passed. The beast spun in consternation. Another dived down, attacking without regards to the safety of its brother. Athan dodged the bite, pulling himself across the dorsal. Where he had been was now a gaping wound, trailing billowing clouds of dark blood. The beast panicked and set off at speed, Athan clinging to the fin with all his strength. The other monsters pursued, their frenzy building with the taste of blood in the water.

Athan saw ahead the jutting masts of a sunken ship. He released his grasp of the dorsal and kicked against the beast's thick flank and descended to the wreck. Eyes wide he glanced over his shoulder to see the predators gaining fast.

The momentum from his kick was dwindling. He swam furiously but could not hope to match the easy grace of the hunters at his heels. Athan closed on a great rib of rotting timber, reaching, finally grasping the edge. With a yell of triumph he pulled himself down into the wreckage. A heartbeat later a pair of jaws rendered the timber into a cloud of splinters. The hunters turned flips in the cold water in frustration as the warlord lay nestled within the shattered hold, panting from the exertion.

With a start he realized he lay in a sailors' grave, a mass of bones amidst the jumble of broken timbers half submerged in sand. The galley slaves were yet chained to their broken oars, bound to the ship even in death. The scavengers of the sea had stripped all their flesh long ago, disturbing their rest and creating a puzzle of their remains. The strange flora of the depths had then sought the bones, coating each with a fuzz of blue green. Here and there skulls lay, mouths open in mute screams.

How terrible a death, silent and hidden from the sun, thought Athan. His reverie was disturbed by the impact of a monster against the ship's broken hull. The predators were not giving up. The warlord knew his shelter would eventually be battered to pieces. His hands disturbed the bones, raising clouds of sediment as he sought a weapon. His soul soared as his hand found a handle. The saber was short and heavy, a weapon for fighting close. The water was filled with the sound of wood splintering as another blow fell upon the hulk.

He watched with keen eyes, corroded blade held ready.

Another hunter descended. Athan sprung up, burying the blade in the beast's underbelly, pulling, opening a gaping wound through which tumbled the beast's foul innards. A great cloud of blood and bile filled the water as the creature thrashed in its death agonies. He dodged another, this time thrusting the old weapon into the creature's left eye, a milky white orb dotted by a soulless black pupil. The eye exploded in a cloud of purple liquid as the beast thrashed, retreating. Its tail, as tall as Athan, battered the warrior back down into the bone strewn remains of the keel.

The presence of so much blood and death wrought chaos in the hunter's ranks. They fell upon each other, turning and snapping with their great maws, a frenzy which degenerated into an orgy of mindless cannibalism. Beyond the savage feast Athan could just make out a shape silhouetted on the surface, a ship. He swam toward the glowing surface of the water, leaving the dire tableau behind, his small body no longer of any interest to the flesh crazed children of the sea witch. He kicked and kicked, water growing brighter the closer to the surface and the blessed rays of the sun.

The warrior surfaced a few feet from the vessel and breathed deep, marveling at the feel of air in his body again. A rope was thrown. He hauled himself onto the deck, a mess of nets and coiled line. The crew, an old skipper and his six sons, stared down in amazement at the warrior, naked as a babe but marked as a raider of the steppe by the looping tattoos that wound their way around his thick chest and arms.

Athan shielded his eyes from the bright sun as he sputtered, "The sea witch, she meant to feed me to her children…"

The skipper interjected, "You see, boys? Have I not

warned you of the sea witch?"

The fishermen had no love of Athan's people but they reckoned his survival below a mark of the gods' favor. The second son rowed the warrior to where his clothes lay. Athan collected his weapons and garments, walking with speed away from the sea witch's beach.

The warlord's steed stamped its hooves in anger at his approach. He watered the impatient creature and stroked the silky mane that lay shining on its proud face. He mounted and galloped east, making for the river. Overhead a pair of wyverns flew in lazy circles, wary of the bow hanging ready next to the rider's saddle. Athan spent a restful night under thick furs pulled tight against the steppe wind.

He rose at dawn and by late morning he had reached the river's edge. Before him lay the barrier, a wall of shimmering blue that reached near as high as the clouds before it faded. He doffed his jacket of iron scale and stripped to the waist, wary of sinking, and drew his sword. He left the horse untethered, knowing his errand may be long. The beast would make its way back to the village.

He pronounced a curse on Thune's soul and waded into the river. The blue light seared his skin immediately. With a shout of pain he dived into the water and paddled through the shallows, vision obscured by swirling clouds of black sediment.

When he could stand his full height he began to walk upright, slogging through the soft mud of the river's bottom. Above him the barrier hovered over the surface, its unearthly light barely penetrating the murky haze.

The grip on his sword tightened as he began to perceive

glowing lights ahead, dots of eerie green piercing the stygian gloom. The lights drew closer and closer. He realized now they were arranged in pairs, luminous eyes set deep into death's heads. The fallen warriors were arrayed in shattered plate and torn mail, bearing each a tall spear and round shield. They surrounded Athan.

A captain spoke in voice like a snake's hiss, "What news of the battle above? We have heard nothing since the Yiure pushed us into the river. Have our armies triumphed? Does High King Hadhzan yet live?"

Athan shook his head. "You speak of the ancient wars between the sorcerer kings and the priest-emperors of the west. The last battle happened long ago, seven times seven times longer than the memory of the oldest elder in the village."

The captain's deathless eyes sought a horizon from distant memory as he replied, "The sorcerer kings made an accord and marched against the Emperor. Hundreds of thousands of men crossed the river. Our boots pounded the world to dust. Our songs echoed from the lowest valley to the highest mountain. Then the armies of white met us on the far bank. The elephants pushed against our shields, driving us back into the water. We tried to fight our way back but a blast of blue light drove us deeper."

Athan was silent.

"What of our King? The terrible Hadzhan, he who rose wyrms from the abyssal depths, he of the black armor…"

"I know not his fate. But all the sorcerer kings died away long ago."

"He was our beloved. None was ever so terrible to behold as our king. We cannot bear to think of him forgotten."

"Hadzhan is the name of many men in my village."

The ghost soldiers looked at each other in turn. Slowly they nodded their rotted heads, terrible visages softened by sentiment.

The captain spoke, "Yes, we see now some of him in you: the gray eyes, the fine features shadowed with cunning and cruelty. Though hidden by the shadow of ages our beloved king lives on…He lives…"

The lights dimmed. Their bodies fell, becoming dust carried now by the gentle current of the dark river.

Athan walked to the far bank.

The coruscating blue brilliance grew in intensity as the water became shallow. The warlord was forced to duck again, finally crawling through the river's muck until he could squeeze between the narrow gap between the water's edge and the barrier. He lay a moment, trading the water in his lungs for sweet scented air.

He stood and inspected his surroundings. A brightness hurt his eyes and he recoiled. Above was a wide blue sky, unmarked with cloud, different than the gray expanse which blanketed the steppe. The sun's warm light illuminated a long plain dotted with wildflowers. Far to the north a forest grew. To the northeast lay a hamlet of stone houses, chimney smoke wafting in the gentle breeze. The air was clean and fresh. No great chasms yawned ahead, dispensing the noxious fumes of the underworld as dotted the steppe. Athan frowned. He found the light oppressive.

A far reflection caught his eye. There in the distance across the forest rose the white towers of legend, the seat of the priest-emperors of old. Athan began walking.

A placid pond lay at the bottom of a slight depression in the plain. The warlord bathed himself. The sound of laughter sent him leaping for his sword where it lay at the pond's edge.

The laughter abruptly ceased as the children crested the low rise and took sight of the warrior. Two girls stood aghast as they inspected Athan. Their garments were simple white tunics without adornment. Athan stared back in annoyance. He sheathed his sword and donned his leather trousers at the water's edge. A look over his shoulder revealed the girls whispering to themselves. One grew bold, stepping forward.

"What are you?"

Athan frowned. Their accent was strange to his ears.

The other girl spoke, "It cannot speak. Come back, Altheali, we must tell the elder."

"I can speak."

The girls gasped, courage failing. They sprinted off toward the village as Athan stared. He finally shook his head and squatted on the grass by the water's edge. There he made an effort to remove the river's sludge that had found its way into every wrinkle of his boots. After a few moments he heard voices in the distance. A party of figures walked purposefully from the village. The group was mostly women, with three large men at the fore, each bearing a pitchfork. The warlord cursed. He had come west for one purpose and one purpose alone, not to treat with farmers or suffer the stares of bizarre foreigners. He began walking.

Strange voices implored he halt. The warlord turned to face the approaching group, hand on the hilt of his sword.

One of the men spoke first, "Hallo, stranger. What manner of being are you?"

Athan's eyebrows raised as he realized he was being addressed by a woman. She was large, larger in fact than him, with close cropped hair and thick features. But she was beardless and soft. Faint impressions of breasts could be seen under her cream colored tunic. The other figures Athan had mistaken for men were the same. Behind them a group of more feminine women huddled in fear.

The warlord held his chin high as he spoke, "I am Athan Bey, Warlord of the Western Steppe, of the Two Wolves Clan." He unconsciously gestured to the crude tattoo scarring his broad chest, two stylized wolves leaping on either side, forever frozen in the moment before their fangs tore each other apart.

The woman answered, "I am Mian, servant of the Priestess. Your accent is strange and you use words that have no meaning. You have the body of a Guardian, one of the white knights, but you have hair on your chin like a shaggy goat and your brow is dark. I do not know what to make of you. Would you consent to come with us back to our village? Like as not the elder will know what you are. Dreams of darkness have rendered her ill. Perhaps you are the thing which will clarify her visions."

Athan thought a moment. For all their bizarreness the people did not seem hostile. And he was very hungry.

"Have you food for me?"

Mian shrugged. "All in the village eat their fill when they are hungry. The Goddess granted us a good harvest last year." She gestured to follow and then turned and began walking. The women walked in clusters ahead, talking and looking back frequently at the strange creature that followed, the thing with hair on its face and marks on its body. Athan felt blood rushing to his face. The warlord was unused to feeling foolish in any way.

The village was a collection of low stone houses

constructed without any particular skill. Some of the thatched roofs had begun to rot, those houses apparently unoccupied. In the center of the village was a crude statue depicting an exaggerated female form, breasts and hips swollen grotesquely. Around the pitted stone were draped floral garlands. At its feet were dishes of food. From the houses more women poured forth. They gave the warrior a wide berth but he was surrounded none the less. Mian gestured for him to sit on the hard packed earth before the statue. A cacophony of whispers rose from the assembled mass. Mian's two companions stood still, flanking Athan at either side.

Athan addressed the one to his left, "Are your men at war?"

She shook her head. "I do not know what those words mean. Do not speak to me. Your voice is like violence."

Athan snorted and shook his head, resigned to being among mad people for the moment. He studied them. They were well favored though perhaps too fair. Each had blonde or light brown hair, cropped short. This detail saved Athan from any pangs of lust. On the steppe hair was shorn close as punishment for bringing dishonor on the clan. The women's skin was pale except where kissed by the sun. Their robes were functional garments, shapeless things of white or cream in color. A few bore infants cradled tight against whatever danger the strange creature in their midst might present.

Athan felt his skin crawl. In his life on the steppe he had only known three kinds of people. There were his tribesmen and their women. There were enemies. And there were slaves. The hierarchy of the village was not without nuance and a certain fluidity. But this situation was beyond the pale. This entire village was for all intents and purposes a women's hut, a place that should have been forbidden to him. The people that surrounded him were not of his people, yet not clearly enemies.

Mian returned, bearing in her thick arms a large bundle of cloth. From one end two thin legs protruded. From the other emerged a face weathered by long years. Her pinched eyes were alight with an intelligence that belied extreme age. Mian set her burden down with care and stepped back. The elder slowly drew her legs underneath her tiny body, tucking them under the folds of coarse linen. Once settled only her face was visible from underneath her hood. The throng grew quiet as they waited for the elder to speak.

Her voice was sharp, a rasping sound that carried much authority.

"What have you brought me?"

Mian replied, "An interloper from the plain. We do not know what it is. It looks like us in some ways but is clearly different. It is somewhat like the guardians that serve the Priestess but clearly not of them. Its face is clouded with hatred and darkness and I recalled your visions of late."

The elder slowly nodded. She leaned forward, squinting. Athan wore a deep scowl.

"I am hungry."

The deep resonance of his voice rippled through the crowd. They stepped back, gasping.

The elder nodded. "Bring gruel."

Athan nodded thanks as a bowl and spoon were set before him. The warlord ate the tasteless sludge as the elder stared.

She spoke again, "It is not a guardian you are right. But it is almost the same. It is a male. I was once a historian in the temple. All the world's secrets are mine."

"Of course I am male. Are there no men here whatsoever?"

The elder shook her head no. "They are a relic of the old age, the age of war. Only the guardians remain. They are oathsworn to serve the Priestess and live in the white temple."

Athan's face betrayed his confusion. "How are children born?"

"Once a year the Priestess visits, carried on a golden palanquin. Her servants use an apparatus, choosing women of the right age, and thus the race continues."

Athan ate wordlessly as the elder continued.

"You have crossed the barrier, have you not?"

"I have."

The crowd erupted with sounds of horror. The elder raised her hand, bony arm slipping from the cloth. Mian shouted for silence. With difficulty the onlookers quieted themselves.

"It is as my dreams foretold. One has come to undo the world."

Athan nodded. "The wizard Thune, a man of my village, said as much. His last breath bade me journey here. I have faced danger and seen strange sights already."

The elder leaned forward. "Were the guardians here now they would slaughter you. But we have no spirit for such violence." With a skeletal hand she waved flies from her face and continued, "Paradise will not be soiled with spilled blood, not here in my village anyway. You must leave now before your presence causes more confusion. Your black aura will draw the weakest away from the path set by the Priestess and all before her. Go now." The elder waved to Mian. "Drape it with the guest's garland and lead it back to the plain. Mourn now, children of the Priestess, if it is what is foretold, we will be the last to walk the path."

Athan stood. "I thank you for the food. By the laws of my

people you may claim protection in my hut, should the need arise."

The elder cackled, "A noble sentiment, male, but as likely to happen as me sprouting wings."

Mian ducked into a house and returned with a garland of white flowers. She placed it around the warlord's neck and gestured for him to follow. A child darted from the crowd, sprinting to stand before Athan. She jumped up to touch his short beard and ran off. The crowd erupted in laughter. A spell had been broken.

As he walked with Mian to the edge of the village the throng closed in. Hands felt his body, the hair on his chest, the breadth of his shoulders, all novelties. They squeezed the hard muscles in his arms and then felt their own for comparison. Their touch was innocent of any lust, a naiveté that allowed them to inspect the warlord's body the way a rider may inspect a horse. Athan bore the indignities will ill grace but controlled his temper. Close to him the women smelled unwashed. Dirt lay under the nails that ran their way through his long hair and beard. He missed the perfumes of the women of the steppe. He missed their long black hair and eyes that showed the same gleam for lust or murder. At the edge of the village the crowd dispersed, seemingly sad for the end of the diversion. Mian bid him goodbye.

"Perhaps you are not the one foretold. Perhaps you will be killed."

Athan met her eyes until she turned away.

The warlord set off for the towers in the distance. A dole of doves from the west passed overhead. He sought omens in the shape of the group but could not hold his eyes to the bright sky long enough. The warlord cursed.

By nightfall he had made it to the forest's edge. Another hamlet lay to the west. Athan had avoided it scrupulously but as he grew close he realized it was abandoned. He entered cautiously. Satisfied it was empty he built a fire in the communal pit and sat before the village's swollen idol. He took the garland from his neck and threw it at the statue's feet then laid to rest. In his dreams he was stalked by figures wrought from shining alabaster. He overcame them, exulting in his victory. Amongst the shards of white lay an arrow. He bent to pick it up only to find it a serpent, striking at his neck.

In the light of dawn the white towers loomed large overhead. The shining rays revealed also their decrepitude. The stones were pitted and streaked with grime. The tops of the highest towers showed jagged lines of stone where the uppermost portions had collapsed. The view was lost as Athan went deeper into the forest.

After the forest lay another plain, and beyond, the temple and its grounds. He could not take his eyes from the towers as he walked in a field of spring wheat. Even in decay the structure was impressive. Athan could not believe people had performed such a feat. Surely he viewed the work of gods. A gasp from nearby startled him. A woman, much the same as Mian, had risen from her work in the field and caught sight of Athan. She gave a muffled cry of surprise and ran toward the temple, imploring her comrades to join her. Others appeared and followed, leaving the warlord standing dumbly, cursing his inattention.

At the end of the field Athan noticed white stone under his feet. The masonry was skillfully wrought but had suffered with the long years.

The warlord felt his apprehension grow. If the guardians

were many and hostile, he would likely die soon. If the prophecy was correct, he might not.

A great door in the center of the largest tower swung open. From out of the darkness within poured a troupe of warriors, knights in gleaming white armor. They marched in step, eyes fixed on Athan. The warlord drew his sword, shaking his head. The knights numbered two dozen. The group passed a large pool of still water dotted with lilies and came to stand before Athan. Their captain eyed him from under a helm crafted in the shape of a graceful swan. A crowd began to gather at the edge of the courtyard, people much like those in the village Athan had visited. Their faces betrayed horror at Athan's arrival and fear of the weapons drawn.

The captain spoke first, "I am Belthi, White Knight of the Temple, Servant of the Priestess, Captain of the Company of the Pure. Are you from beyond the barrier?"

"I am Athan Bey, Warlord of the Western Steppe, of the Two Wolves Clan. I have come from across the barrier as compelled by prophecy."

"Is the prophecy from the Goddess?"

"I know not your Goddess. The prophecy comes from the gods of Change and Death, related to me by Thune the Cursed, Thune the Mushroom Eater."

"Then so goes your last chance to live. Your very presence here is an affront to the Goddess. Your soul will be doubly cursed for forcing me to spill blood in paradise."

Athan's eyes looked past the captain to the tower's doorway. There stood a woman of incomparable beauty. Her green eyes sat calm under a delicate brow. From temple to cheek, to mouth and chin, the lines of her face described an impossible perfection. Her beauty was all things at once, chaste and lustful, mournful and blissful, fleeting and eternal.

She was the earth's rhythms, the lust of spring, the excess of summer, the remorse of fall, the sorrow of winter. She was the Priestess. Alone among the Ullin she wore her hair long. The wind stirred the fair locks to alight on cheek and shoulder. Athan's heart ached to look upon her.

The business at hand brought him back to face the captain.

"Is it to be a duel or will you and your dogs advance upon me at once?"

The captain answered crisply, "I will fight you. Say a prayer to the wretched gods of your people. Woe to you, to have seen paradise before death!"

Belthi advanced behind his shield, sword held aloft. Athan gave ground, studying his foe. He had never fought a man in so much armor before. In his head began the animal calculations of the natural fighter. He saw every one of Belthi's movements in minute detail, a crystal clarity honed by the threat of death. He watched without watching, his attention spread evenly to his whole opponent before him, eyes resting around the shifting center. His subconscious factored everything, including his own movements as his hard body moved sometimes in response, sometimes to provoke a response. The captain essayed the first strike, confident in his thick broadsword and heavy armor. The blade whistled harmlessly past as Athan ducked.

The warlord aimed a probing blow upwards as he stood, catching the captain near the waist. His blade chipped the heavy plate, a result neither expected. Belthi struck again, a downward swing that Athan parried, moving to nullify the force of the blow and save his blade against the full force of the broadsword. His follow through tipped Belthi forward. With a viper's speed Athan lashed out with a vicious swing at the captain's neck. The knight sunk slightly, catching the blow on his thick helm. The cheek plate shattered, revealing half the smooth, hairless face underneath. Belthi raised a gauntleted hand to feel his face while Athan circled. The captain brought his shield up, taking a more defensive posture, chastened by the break in his helm. The two traded blows, parrying with their blades. Belthi now gave ground. Athan gained strength from the knight's fear as bats on the steppe gained strength from the blood of sleeping horses on moonless summer nights.

He aimed a heavy blow down on Belthi's shield and dodged the counter swing which followed. The shield came apart in the captain's grasp. Athan's soul filled with elation. The man's armor and shield must be ancient, gone brittle with the passing of centuries. Belthi cast aside the remains of his shield and summoned his courage. He lunged forward. The warlord knocked aside the thrust with his blade and kicked heartily at Belthi's exposed torso. The captain fell sprawling on the stones, bits of his armor coming apart with the impact. Athan swung again as the captain righted himself. The helm shattered completely. The white knights grew agitated. They broke ranks, crowding in on the fight. Athan had eyes only for Belthi. The captain stood dazed. Athan struck.

Blood pumped from the severed neck as the body lay twitching. The warlord reached down and grasped the bald head by its stump. Around him the spectators sent up a wail of anguish and disgust, many losing consciousness from the horror of it. He raised his trophy in triumph. At the moment of his exultation a blow smashed the back of his head. He blacked out, waking moments later and finding the white knights holding him firm as he knelt on the ground. They wept as they looked to the Priestess.

One spoke finally, "Milady?"

The Priestess' face betrayed no emotion as she spoke, "Kill him. But shed no more blood."

Athan was nearly insensate but still protested. "No! I am victorious! The prophecy..."

The white knights dragged him into the lily pool. Two held each arm as a third grasped his legs and a fourth held a handful of Athan's hair and pushed his head under the murky water. He strained against their grip as an animal the moment before slaughter. The cool liquid brought sense back to the warlord. He breathed deep, laughing as they held him, soon warming to playing the part of a drowning man. He thrashed furiously against their hold and then went limp in their arms.

Another white knight of evident rank spoke, "Throw his corpse in the refuse pit and prepare Belthi for burial."

Athan let his breath come as shallow as he could as they carried him. The white knights wound their way along a path that led to the edge of a slope shrouded by low trees. They tossed their burden into the muck. He listened as they left, armor clinking as they walked with a step made heavier by the loss of their comrade. When he was certain they were out of earshot he took in a hearty lungful of air and laughed out loud.

The sky above was taking on a purple tone, the beginning of dusk. The smell of waste filled his nostrils as he crawled up the bank.

He waited for the fullness of night, hidden amongst the trees. As darkness fell the villagers retired and the knights were seen no more. High above in the tallest tower a light shone from a wide balcony.

## Athan and the Priestess

The worn stone offered easy purchase. He scaled in silence, sweat erupting the length of his hard body. He dared not look down. Life on the steppe had offered no opportunity to test one's courage against the fear of falling. His goal neared as his arms burned with the long exertion. With a panther's grace he slid over the balcony's stone rail.

He stood in the Priestess' private apartments. In the center of the room she bathed in a bronze tub. Tendrils of steam rose toward the arched ceiling, carrying with them the scent of jasmine. She became still suddenly, sensing his presence. She turned.

"So, it is you. You live, somehow. The cup bearer of death has ascended the white tower."

"You know the prophecy?"

She stood and stepped from the bath, dripping water onto a carpet woven with images of the tower in its glorious past. Moisture wafted from the contours of her body in the gentle cool of the Ullin night.

Athan spoke again, "You know why I am here."

"I do. I and all my predecessors have known this day would come. All things must end. Truthfully, I welcome it. When one day is as the next the soul shrinks, colors become gray, the scent of flowers becomes stale. Since my birth I have dutifully walked the path set before me. But it all ends now."

Athan could look at her no longer. He reached forward to take her hand.

She pulled him instead. "I must bathe you first."

He settled into the water as she directed. She stood above him dousing him with oil and setting to work, first rinsing the grime from his hair, then his face. Her hands were strong despite their softness as they worked over his hard body, so

41

different than hers yet of the same thing. His form was hard where hers was soft, dark where hers was light, rough where hers was smooth. The tension left his body as she worked. He stared at her face, transfixed.

Though her hand trembled her step was sure as she led him to the bed. The warrior proceeded with care, mindful of her inexperience. She held onto his broad back tightly until the pain subsided. Athan moved with the languid pace of lapping waves, slowly building with force as he felt her body responding, hips moving to meet his, matching his hunger. She whispered in his ears words he could not understand. He rolled, leading her to sit atop him, hands guiding her hips, silently instructing her in the ways the women of the steppe guaranteed their own pleasure. It is believed there that sons are born from women who feel the pleasure most. She found her rhythm and soon was awash in ecstasy. He finished soon after.

They lay together a moment before he rose. Athan did not look back, fearing his heart would break and he would be unmanned.

Two days later he emerged from the under the barrier. He smiled to see his horse had waited. He carried his tale back to his people where he became known as Athan Water Breather and Athan Slayer of the White Knight. Two summers later he was felled by an arrow to the neck.

The Priestess bore a son, the first born in such a way in centuries. The father's blood was strong in the child. But the ways of learning, passed from the Priestess, were just as strong. In the fullness of time the child grew into a powerful sorcerer. He brought down the barrier and subjugated the villages east and west of the river. He broke the backs of the nomads and shattered the white towers. He raised cities from the dust and prised forgotten alphabets from the mouths of the dead. The gods would learn his name and become again interested in the affairs of man. Death and Change congratulated themselves as they watched all unfold from the eyes of ravens.

But those are stories for another time.

# The Movements of the Ige

It was the joyous time, the time for dancing and killing amongst the Ige. The red moon was ascendant over its green sibling and now stood in front of the second sun. The killing season had begun. Overhead the thur circled on their leathery wings, describing auspicious patterns in their lazy arcs across the swirling orange sky.

The group of Ige who called themselves the Ar arrayed themselves for war and marched to the field. The group who called themselves the Ya would meet them and then the slaughter would begin. As legend went, the Ar and Ya were spawned from the same egg. But in its eternal wisdom, the god-sun had made sibling war against one another. The Ige wrote poetry with the movement of their powerful long bodies. Their oily black green scales would gleam in the waning ochre light as they spun and hacked. Great wounds would gush bright green blood and many would sing their death song, directing their droning melodies up at the crimson disc. Thus amongst the Ige neither the Ar nor the Ya ever bred in numbers to tax the herd. Such was the cruel symmetry imposed by the god-sun upon the world called Igemid. The Ige known to his brothers as Kor, of the Ar group, walked at the head of the horde.

Like many of his siblings, Kor was superficially male but sterile, now sixteen cycles old and fully grown, broad of chest and tall, vain, and proud of his tail. The severe angles and perfect symmetry of his face and its scales were highly regarded. The warrior also had an abundance of the characteristics the Ar held in esteem; he was graceful and quick to recognize beauty. He was also incredibly cruel. With such qualities he was chosen as Ar-chief and wore a necklace of skulls as symbol of the office. It was the only ornament any of the Ar wore.

Kor surveyed the field with pupils slit vertically. The warrior warmed his throat, preparing his death song as he watched the Ya dance, spinning their obsidian blades in great arcs. It was Kor's third battle and the warrior felt in his heart that he would finally meet his long awaited death. He would feed the scuttling things with his corpse on this day and they would grow fat and slow. They would be gathered in baskets by the females after a few cycles and the largest would be put aside. The females, immortal and haughty beings, would crack the smooth carapaces with sharp rocks. With their graceful hands they would implant their eggs deep into the soft organs of the scuttling things, all the while singing their lilting hymns to the god-sun. From such beginnings the next generation would grow and spawn and be strong like Kor.

The warrior delighted in the knowledge of the pattern. Weapon hand, shield hand. Mountains and plains. Suns and moons. Life and death. Thusly the god-sun made the world. Kor's heart beat with joy.

# The Movements of the Ige

The chief and his brothers peered across the plain at the Ya and hurled insults. The Ya shook their heads, hissing in rage. The killing time was approaching. Now was the pregnant moment. In this time all was seen as the first time. Kor saw his brothers, saw their strength and murderous grace as they danced. Soon the vision would be awash in blood and then finally blackness. Kor spared a glance toward the god-sun shining in the sky. The warrior prayed it would be pleased by their movements. The two sides advanced past the stele that past generations had erected in the field.

But the Ya were stopping. The enemy warriors had ceased their movements and all looked upward. Their careful rhythms and complex movements had been interrupted.

Kor addressed his brothers. "What is the meaning of this?" The Ar reluctantly ceased their own movements.

Tij followed their gaze and nudged Kor, pointing upward. Up in the sky an object was suspended in the air, a rounded gray cylinder of a length many times the height of a warrior. The object was spinning slowly and descending. It trailed a length of black smoke behind it.

"What is that?"

"I do not know. But it has spoiled the battle. All our dancing is come to naught." Kor called out to his enemy. "Ya-chief. I would speak with you!"

Across the field, the Ya-chief answered. "I will speak with you." Both cast down their shields, black circles of fire hardened shell from the crawlers that lurked in the mountain caves.

They met in the middle of the barren field. The object still flew. Its speed seemed to decrease as it neared the surface some distance away.

The Ya-chief spoke first. "The battle is interrupted. My

movements were approaching a crescendo but the object destroyed my trance. My heart is broken."

"Mine too. What is that object which interrupted us and took our minds from the god-sun's will?"

"I could not guess."

Kor watched the object disappear behind a line of hills. "I wish to know what it is."

The Ya-chief waved his hand over his own face, a gesture of negation. "I do not. When next the killing moon rises again we will meet."

Mournful wails filled the plain as the Ya left the field. The Ar-chief addressed his horde.

"I go now to find out what is the object which interrupted us."

Tij shook his clawed hand before his face. "The activity seems pointless. I return to the village to practice my movements and drink fermentation."

Most of the horde followed him. Standing with Kor now were a dozen of the younger warriors. They were tentative in their movements and availed themselves of every opportunity to observe Kor whom they loved. Ruj was the oldest among them, nearly as tall as Kor and also bearing a fine face and thick, powerful legs and arms.

The Ar-chief set out toward the hills with the dozen following. The red moon sank, revealing a sliver of the second sun behind. The killing time was nearly over. No corpses littered the field, a disappointment that the females would note in sharp tones.

As they walked some of the young warriors made movements for the others' approval but Kor's heart was too heavy to join them.

The hills grew closer. Traces of smoke lingered where the

object had fallen. Kor ordered stealth.

The group crawled to the crest of the hill. Below in the shallow gulley the object sat. It was long and shaped like an egg pulled from either end. The thing was textured with areas of sharp angles, gray in color like granite but largely smooth. It stood on three legs, thin stalks of oily sliver terminating in wide, flat feet. It was like nothing ever seen on Igemid.

A flash of movement quickened Kor's heart. Around from the other side walked a figure like an Ar but smaller. Its gray skin was bloated and wrinkled and it bore one great eye in the center of its head. The eye reflected all around it with a copper tint. The thing moved around the egg, touching, prodding, with apparent haste. Kor hissed. The warriors lying near him stirred. The Ar-chief's mind raced.

There was a gasping sound from the egg. Suddenly a portal slid open and another creature emerged, stepping down a ladder to alight on the ground.

Ruj whispered, "Their movements are graceless."

Kor answered, "Indeed. What creatures are these? They interrupted our battle and here they walk around their great egg without the merest cast of remorse or conciliatory stance. Their posture is arrogant, especially after such an affront."

Ruj pondered. "Perhaps the egg dictates their movements."

"I do not think so. I sleep in a hut. The hut bears no intelligence. I think the egg is a hut."

"That fell from the sky?"

"Perhaps they are demons from the red moon. Their domicile became dislodged and they fell to this world."

Ruj shrugged. "The theory is sound. I grow tired of lying here watching the wrinkled ones. Even demons must pay their debts. These here stole away the language of my body on the death-plain, patterns and rhythms that are lost to that moment, never to be expressed to completion. A thousand more killing moons could not recreate that instance."

Ruj stood and walked down the hill. With a smooth motion he brought his obsidian blade from its sling on his back. The creatures milled about below, unawares. Kor cursed. He had wanted more time to ponder but Ruj had acted correctly, heedless of death and contemptuous of mystery. With a panicked start one of the creatures noticed Ruj's approach. Its fat hands fumbled at its waist. With a spinning leap Ruj closed the gap and brought his jagged blade down upon the thing. Its head split in a shower of red and glittering shards of material that shined like crystal. The other creature pointed his hand at Ruj. There was a great noise, like a boulder falling, and Ruj's beautiful head became a green mist. Kor and the other warriors were given heart by the sight of death. They sped down the hill, lungs bursting with song and legs bounding. Another two warriors were struck down by the ineffable force of the creature's hand. Kor struck it with his fist and the thing flew, tumbling into the dirt. It shot back to its feet and scrambled to the portal. Kor felt his soul soar. He was spattered with his brothers' blood and moving, twisting in practiced patterns. The thing scurried into the portal. The door slid shut, stopped at the last moment by the Ar-chief's blade. The creature stuck its hand out the gap. Kor grasped the hand and crushed it. A tiny egg of black, bearing a short handle, fell from the creature's grasp. The other warriors wrenched the portal open as the creature scurried deeper into the egg. Kor dove into the portal after it.

## The Movements of the Ige

Inside was bizarreness. First another portal was passed through. Then Kor found himself inside the egg. Yu, one of the younger warriors, followed close behind. A thousand tiny suns shined in the cramped interior, arrayed against the irregular walls. Some blinked, others showed displays of light and form that made no sense to the Ar's eyes. The creature lay on the floor, crawling backwards. Kor raised his blade but stayed his hand. Yu urged him on.

"Kill it and let us be done with this. We will drag the corpses back to the field and the tur will feed after all."

"You may do so. I wish to observe this thing. Something of import transpires."

"I wonder these actions will corrupt your movements. Crawling things without grace poke and prod to satisfy curiosity."

Kor made a gesture that conveyed imminent violence. Two fingers raised, the middle finger folded to his palm and thumb outstretched. He moved the hand across his face. Yu stepped back and continued, "Your pervasive force and immense beauty grant you latitudes in conduct. I apologize."

Kor turned back to observe the creature. It had pulled itself into a sitting position upon a protuberance and its fat fingers worked along one of the sun panels. Suddenly the egg was filled with sound, the voice of an Ar, familiar yet odd.

"No kill."

Yu reeled. "The egg speaks?"

Kor shook his head. "It is the creature. I believe it manipulates the egg to make speech. We will test this theory." Kor addressed the creature, "Why did you interrupt our movements?"

The voice rang out again in its odd tone, flat and without emotion. "Accident. Apology. No kill."

51

Kor laughed. "If we take the creature at its word then at least we know our battle was not ruined by malign intent." The creature worked the panels again. It cradled its crushed hand in its lap as the other hand worked.

"Leave now. Fixed. Ready. Go and no return. Apologies."

Yu fidgeted. "I am satisfied. Kill it. I cannot move properly here. My heart grows heavy."

"Calm yourself. We know nothing as yet. What thing is this egg? What manner of creature is this and why is it here?" He turned to the creature, "What are you?"

The creature seemed to struggle at the panel.

The voice sounded. "Watcher. From place far away. Not Igemid."

Yu wailed. "Madness!"

Kor's beautiful face twisted into a mask of puzzlement. "Another place? You are demons then?"

"Not demons. Watching. Studying. Accident. Apologies. No kill."

"This egg enables you to travel?"

"Yes. Far into sky."

Yu made for the portal. "I can stand no more."

Kor was alone with the creature.

"So you have seen the god-sun and the eternal dancers which move through the sky?"

"Yes."

"The Ar dance to please the god-sun and express its will in motion. Our lives express harmonies made complete with death. You will take me, in this egg, to meet the god-sun. I will study its divine movements with my own eyes."

The creature hesitated at the panel. Kor became annoyed. His tail whipped the air.

The voice sounded, "No."

Kor became enraged. "Your egg interrupted the battle. Your presence caused me to display a curiosity that diminished my aura in the beautiful eyes of my brothers. Now you dare refuse my request. I will flay you and create secret angles with the arcs of your blood across the sky, inside which are glimpsed places where time, death, and life intersect. I will make a rhythm with the cracking of your bones. I will cast your corpse into fire so no scuttling thing eats of it and grows large enough to host." Kor grabbed the creature by the arm. Its free hand reached desperately for the panel.

"Yes. See god-sun. No kill."

Kor released the creature. It went from one panel to the next, touching the tiny suns. The portals slid shut. There was a great humming sound, unpleasant, then the feeling of motion though Kor's feet were firm on the floor of the egg. The creature depressed a final sun and Kor stared in wonder as a panel slid away. He could see mountains in the distance and the great plains where the herd ambled. The two suns shone in the direction of his shield side. The egg gathered speed. Igemid shrank underneath as they flew. Kor kept his eyes fixed on the portal. The world below became a great band of bright tan at his shield side. Upwards they continued.

Ahead now was the god-sun, surrounded by blackness dotted with the shining lights of the eternal dancers. Kor's heart swelled. The god-sun grew in size but then the egg ceased suddenly.

"Why have we stopped?"

"Danger. No more close. Danger."

The Ar-chief's scales shined opalescent in the pale light of the egg's interior as his muscles rippled across his body.

"My patience is exhausted."

Kor's hand lashed forward. The brittle surface of the creature's great eye shattered as his fist punched through into the flesh underneath. The red blood of the creature flowed in great gouts from the wound and it collapsed on the floor in a heap of wrinkled gray  and small limbs. Kor touched the panels as he observed the creature had done. The touch of his claws disturbed the egg. The broken panel spat sparks in anger. The egg lurched forward, faster this time. Several of the small suns glowed red as the egg began to scream, a pulsing, unpleasant noise. Kor lashed out with his tail at the place from where the sound originated and the egg grew quiet again.

The god-sun grew larger as the egg's interior became hot. Kor watched as it swelled into the whole of his view, a universe of blinding light and fury. Great tendrils of fire danced in violent arcs, lashing out and falling back down, again and again.

The beauty of it broke Kor's heart. He sang a song of mourning and exultation as the egg was incinerated.

# The Ecology
# of the Unicorn

Malathiksos stood at the rail, feeling his joints stiffen in the bracing autumn winds that whispered of coming winter. He left the balcony and ordered the imps to make a fire. The sorcerer made himself comfortable in a low slung chair made from the bones of a wyvern as he pondered his predicament over a goblet of mulled wine.

Death was approaching. He had seen a rider shrouded in wisps of faded black haunting the grounds of his estates on three occasions in the last weeks. The rider grew bolder each time, lingering closer and closer to his front door, a three storied thing embossed with a catalog of his victories over time and matter.

The sorcerer ordered a lectern brought forth and spent the evening poring over a series of dusty tomes. The research revealed nothing he did not already know. Neither his predecessors nor other sorcerers in his correspondence had been able to do naught but stave off death for a time once the rider had been sighted.

The sorcerer had already exhausted all of the known tricks to extend his life through the long centuries necessary to master his craft. He had fashioned hourglasses that turned hours into months. He had imbibed revitalizing tonics made from dew gathered from the world's first morning. Pacts made with ill-tempered things from planes of smoke and noise had long since expired. The harvester's arrival was imminent. Malathiksos' life dipped like a stalk of wheat, heavy in its fullness and awaiting the scythe.

He tested his own ability to accept the inevitable. Few things across the whole of the nine planes lived longer than a sorcerer of worth. He supposed he should be grateful for his time. He tore the thought from his mind like one might cast off an ill fitting garment.

Down winding stairwells Malathiksos walked, scattering imps before him. He entered his menagerie. A cold stare silenced the gloating caw of a plumed thung imprisoned behind bars of cursed jade. He opened a cabinet and removed a brass cage in which reclined a fae, napping on a bed of straw.

"Awake, Rutu. I wish to ask a question."

The fae rubbed sleep from his yellow eyes. "I shall answer nothing until you agree to free me."

"You will answer my question or I will suspend this cage in boiling water."

"How utterly mundane! I fear the long years have eroded your creativity. Could this be the same sorcerer who made the Black Tarot that caused poor Tretius to walk under the shadow of a thousand ill-omens? It is said the watercolors are exquisite, so beautiful that to look upon them is a worthy trade for utter doom. Painted by your own hand, no? And now you threaten me with hot water!"

"Your words are true and thus injurious. I can write no poetry in death's shadow. So you must tell me, how are the fae immortal? Few other creatures in the universe are as long lived. There must be a reason."

Rutu sat crossed legged, pointed chin resting on hand. "I do not know for sure. But I believe our playfulness, our natural exuberance and joyful demeanor, perhaps these things account for our immortality. You should try it. Leave now and find a tavern where you can dance to a bard's tune. Gather poesies in a field and spend time remarking on the natural beauty you see around you. Your new outlook would reinvigorate those tired bones and keep the rider at bay."

Malathiksos beckoned an imp forward and ordered a pot of water brought to boil in the kitchen.

Rutu spoke, "Come now, gray beard. My advice is sincere. And you cannot really expect me to divulge such secrets."

The sorcerer carried the cage with him down the long stone staircase to the tower's kitchen.

The fae remonstrated. "What you ask I cannot say."

"You must, or be boiled."

"I am oathsworn to silence. Perhaps though..."

The sorcerer's eyebrows arched. "Perhaps what?"

"I may not deliberately divulge this information. But who knows what a careless act might reveal? Take me to your library. To assuage my boredom I will peruse a volume or two. In my carelessness I might leave a book open. It's just the type of thing I am wont to do. My own private chambers in the tree at Illylisily are the very picture of disorder. By random chance the open leaf may contain information useful to yourself. Stranger things have been known to happen."

Malathiksos altered course. He entered a long hallway lined with sculpture, each a warrior frozen in attitudes of defense; the victims of a basilisk. The oak doors of his library opened at his approach revealing a cylindrical chamber stretching far upwards. A pair of long armed apes looked up from a book they shared, a colorful folio. They snapped to attention at their master's approach. The sorcerer addressed the fae.

"What book would you care to see?"

"Mundy's Taxonomy of Beasts."

The sorcerer raised an eyebrow. "Indeed? Such a common work."

"Please do not press me. This pretense must be maintained."

Malathiksos nodded to the apes. They leapt up, swinging from tier to tier with an easy grace. One paused at the second floor. The other shot upward then horizontally, scanning the shelves as he swung, fingers walking along the bowed spines of the hidebound tomes as his eyes narrowed in concentration. After backtracking once the primate found his mark, pulling the book free and tossing it down to his fellow. Book underarm, the ape swung down. With a reverent bow he placed the tome on the table.

Malathiksos addressed the fae, "This does not mean your freedom, only that you avoid the cauldron for today."

"Generosity is another trait that may work wonders to improve the quality and length of life. From your sour expression I see I waste words."

The sorcerer whispered a syllable under his breath and the cage became unlocked. Rutu hopped to the table. With both hands he strained against the cover. Malathiksos nudged the fae aside with a careful motion, fingers pressed against the tiny back, and opened the book. Rutu looked up at the sorcerer.

"Our pretense?"

Malathiksos made a gesture of impatience. He left the

library, shutting the heavy doors behind him, and placed his gnarled ear to the wood.

He faintly heard pages flipping then a sound he could not recognize. The pointed toes of his shoes were suddenly awash in blue light, exploding from the gap between the door and the dressed stone underfoot. A thunderclap followed. With an oath the sorcerer burst through the doors.

At the sill of the shattered window he watched Rutu escaping. The fae sat on the spine of a book, cover and pages flapping in imitation of a bird. The apes emerged from hiding and peered around their master at the flying book and rider. The two groaned; the fae had enchanted the volume they had been reading, their favorite book, now flying forever out of reach. Tears welled in their eyes.

Malathiksos retrieved a set of thick goggles from a pocket in his red robes. Through the lens' he could see the trail of star dust glowing in the fae's wake, material deposited onto the creature's back by the sorcerer's own fingers mere moments ago. The secret path to Illylisily was now clear as day.

On the table Mundy's Taxonomy lay open. Malathiksos looked at the entry.

"Unicorns. Native to the forests surrounding Illylisily. These creatures...." The entry elaborated on the ecology of the unicorn, facts well known to the sorcerer. There was nothing in the entry explaining their legendary immortality. What secrets did the fae keep regarding this creature of their forest?

An ape tugged at his embroidered sleeve, handing forth a slip of paper. Malathiksos read the title, written in a scrawling, sloppy hand.

"*Prince Minoj and the Suffocating Curves of Sultana and*

Schuyler Hernstrom

*Her Jealous Sisters. A poem in 40 stanzas with Accompanying Illustrations.*"

The sorcerer patted the ape on its broad head. "Yes, yes, I shall order another copy."

Malathiksos ordered an imp to saddle his prize moth and set off immediately. The great beast was slow in the crisp autumn air as far below the sorcerer's estates gave way to farmland dotted with villages, long rolling plains broken by orchards and copses of wood reserved for game. The Krixxis mountains loomed ahead, an old range worn smooth by wind and rain. On the highest peak the jutting metal ribs of an ancient hulk marked the point where it had fallen from the stars many eons ago.

The trail of star dust led to an intersection between planes, a landmark only visible to sorcerers or cats. Malathiksos guided the moth through the narrow opening to emerge in a realm of purple fog and arcing energies. The mist cleared to reveal a wide forest. Atop a low hill rose Green House, the largest tree in Illylisily. Its trunk bulged with the faes' improvements, doors and windows, gables and alcoves, ringed with walkways and bridges connecting its many apartments.

Malathiksos followed the trail to a clearing west of the great tree where wildflowers dotted a lawn of verdant grass. In the center of the meadow Rutu lay on a blanket while another fae fed him fruit from a woven basket. The pair watched the moth's descent with widening eyes. The grass shimmered as it undulated under the gentle gusts of the beast's purple and gray wings. The girl ran off as Rutu howled in anger.

"My picnic is ruined! The long years of my captivity were

60

spent in imagining just this event; a simple meal of fruit and cheese, enlivened by the company of a lovely young woman. Despite the unseasonable cold it was going along swimmingly. And now you have spoiled it!" Rutu looked up at the sorcerer and continued, "But however did you find your way here?"

Malathiksos climbed down from the saddle as he replied. "I followed you here, how else? A mere touch of star dust was all it took."

Rutu's face took on an unhealthy pallor. "So, it is my fault tranquility is destroyed."

"Indeed. Well, what's done is done."

"Why have you come anyway? What was it you wanted?"

"The secret of the fae's immortality, you halfwit! Linked somehow to the unicorn, as you indicated by way of the book."

"You are a monomaniac. It is off-putting in the extreme."

Malathiksos shrugged. "If you would simply give me what I need then I would trouble you no more."

Rutu threw up his hands. He was searching for words when the blaring of a shrill trumpet directed their attention up the gentle slope toward the great tree.

The fae shook his head. "Your presence has been noted. The king will not look kindly on my role in this breach. Your emprise may cost us both our lives."

Down charged the hussars, sabers held ready, pelisses fluttering in the cool air. In a display of classic élan the mounts were being pushed to their limits, their jerking, side to side gait near violent enough to throw the riders from off their scaled backs.

Malathiksos raised his hands in a gesture of submission while Rutu stood, eyes downcast. The hussars surrounded the pair, bringing their hissing mounts under control with some difficulty. Once still the mounts seem to enter a torpor.

An officer, set off from the others by an overabundance of gold braid draped across his shoulders, addressed the sorcerer.

"I am Captain Ghintu of the King's Own. Please identify yourself and explain your presence here."

The sorcerer made a curt bow and introduced himself. "I am Malathiksos, 43$^{rd}$ of the Order, Conjurer and Painter of Tarot. I journeyed to this realm in order to study the ecology of the unicorn."

"And with you is Rutu."

"Yes, cousin. This grim scholar held me prisoner for 83 years until I won free by a spectacular display of cleverness. Then he followed me here."

"Followed, or was led?"

Rutu grimaced, color flooding his cheeks as he answered, "See here, now! Often in the past my esteemed countrymen have mistaken my natural joie de vivre for irresponsibility or perhaps a lack of morals. But to accuse me of revealing the location of the Great Tree? It is an obscenity to imagine that I have forsworn that most sacred of oaths! Were I armed, and well rested and properly exercised, I may have considered demanding satisfaction from you for that remark!"

The captain shook his head. "Oh, cousin. You are back for not yet a full hour and already you have become utterly tiresome. Only pity for my aunt stays my hand."

Malathiksos interrupted, "Perhaps I should begin my investigations and leave you both to your reunion."

The captain looked up. "I am afraid my orders are to kill you, as you are a most unwelcome interloper."

"You may find the task difficult."

"Are you warded against physical attack?"

The sorcerer replied, "Of course I am. No weapons except blades chilled to absolute zero or those wielded by beings of unblemished good can harm me."

"Would you permit me to verify this? Pardon my incredulity, I certainly mean no offence."

"I quite understand." Malathiksos main a plaintive gesture with his hands and took a step away from Rutu. The captain nodded to a subordinate. The fae took a dagger from his belt and tossed it into the air. He caught it by the blade and then hurled it toward the sorcerer. The tiny knife sped toward its target only to bounce harmlessly off an invisible barrier.

The captain of the hussars made a gesture of defeat.

"I consider my duties discharged to the best of my ability. I wish you both good day." He snapped the reins, stirring the mount back to alertness. The beast hissed in anger. The captain turned in the saddle and spoke, "I will say this; make your investigations quickly. I will have to make a thorough report upon returning to the tree. Our wizards will learn your name and consult their almanacs and "who's who's" to learn of you and your possible weaknesses. They will use their mortegraph to attempt contact with long deceased family or friends to learn your secret names and compromising details. They will encumber disposable apprentices with weighty spells and send them in waves to kill you."

Malathiksos looked from under hooded eyes as he replied, "I give you much thanks for the warning. But why? Why tell me all this?"

"I despise our wizards. It is not enough they must beat one in chess or word plays. They have to gloat so!" The captain gestured with a sweep toward his own person and continued, "Behold my skill in the saddle, my splendid uniform and gleaming saber! Note the rakish effect of my hat set off to one side. See how the maroon stripe on my boots matches the color of the pelisse, creating a harmonious ensemble. Does one suppose this is all accident? Is there a more splendid regiment anywhere in the nine realms? It means nothing to them! They send me trotting down the hill to observe how you kill me, to gain intelligence! A disgrace."

The sorcerer raised his hand, pleading a moment's more patience. "Captain, if you would, please. A gift for your wizards. A rare gem. Perhaps it will make them less ill disposed toward me." From a pouch at his waist Malathiksos produced a rough cut ruby, as big as a plum. The bright sunlight which flooded the meadow seemed to illuminate tongues of flame dancing in its core. He bent low to hand it to the captain who took it in both arms, nearly hiding his annoyance at the burden.

"I doubt it. You are the first mortal man to find his way to these lands. Their security is forever compromised. But I will let them know you seem to mean no ill."

Silver spurs sent his mount pelting up the hill as fast as its sinuous gait would allow. The regiment followed.

Rutu let out a long sigh of relief. "I yet live."

Malathiksos hunched his thin shoulders against a sudden gust of chill air. "And so do I. According to Mundy's, unicorns gather amidst the Sacred Pool which lies in a clearing ringed by old oak."

Rutu laughed. "Sacred Pool? There are dozens of locations. Essentially, every pool in Illylisily is a 'Sacred Pool'."

"I believe I spy oaks to the west. I shall head that way.

While I have you, would you care to impart any addition information?"

"About what?"

The sorcerer spoke through clenched teeth, "The link between unicorns and immortality."

"Ah, yes." He paused, scratching his chin. His lips curled into a wry smile as he looked up at Malathiksos. "Well, as you doubtless recall, I am forbidden to speak of it."

"Oh really, Rutu, what harm could it do at this point? I outwitted you with pitiable ease and you led me here to this place. Me, the first mortal to walk here. The first to find his way to Illylisily. Is that not more significant than anything else? I confess, I dabbed you as mere insurance. I did not imagine for an instant that you would lead me directly here. I mean, just think on it for a moment, the location of Great Tree, Green House, one of the great secrets of the universe. Undone! By your haste to enjoy a picnic and a tussle with a beautiful fae girl! Its incredible!"

Rutu's face drained of color for a moment then warm crimson blossomed on his high cheeks. He sputtered a syllable or two, grasping for words as a spasm crawled spiderlike across his delicate features. His healthy color returned slowly as he breathed deep. Finally he seemed to possess again his easy equanimity, spoiled slightly by a untoward gleam in the eyes.

He replied in amiable tones, "Yes, I suppose you are right. Indeed, what harm could it possibly cause? First let us make for that stand of oak."

Malathiksos smiled, thin lips peeled across his small, sharp teeth, and spoke, "Yes, you see reason finally. Let us walk briskly. I see the great tree disgorges itself of wizards' apprentices."

Inside the shadowed wood the air had grown even cooler. Rutu sat atop the sorcerer's shoulder while the old man negotiated a terrain of gnarled root and small granite boulders.

"Up ahead!'"

Malathiksos replied, gasping, "Yes, I see it."

Before them lay a placid pool ringed by flowers. A break in the cover above permitted a ray of sunshine to bathe the area in clarity and warmth. The pool reflected the cloudless sky above, a plane of perfect blue, broken only occasionally by the flight of a bird.

And there, just in the shadows, idled a unicorn. The proud creature chewed a mouthful of clovers as it watched the interlopers from the side, stepping away.

"Oh no, we're disturbing it."

"Easy, gray beard. Take it slow. You are lucky. It is a male. These creatures mate for life, rendering the males placid and complaisant."

Malathiksos looked to his shoulder, whispering his question. "And what exactly am I supposed to do?"

Rutu smiled. "Ah, yes. You need simply touch it. Unicorns are the embodiment of purity and goodness and life. The merest touch is all that is needed to ward off the rider for centuries."

The sorcerer grinned, "Splendid!"

"Shhh! Slowly now…"

Malathiksos crept closer to the unicorn which now turned to inspect him openly. The beast shook its head slightly, tail swishing, stepping back again.

"I don't think he likes me."

"Of course he doesn't. You are a servant of selfish evil. But just another step or two."

# The Ecology of the Unicorn

With a crying neigh the unicorn bolted. Malathiksos' narrow shoulders sagged.

"So close! Alas, it will be a chore following him. But don't they always travel in pairs?"

"Yes, yes they do."

There was a crash as the other unicorn burst through the brush. The mare leapt toward the sorcerer, head lowered. The old conjurer could not even turn in time.

Malathiksos looked down. From just beneath his sternum a horn slathered in red black gore protruded. The mare stepped back, unsheathing its horn from the sorcerer's torso. With a groan the man crumpled to the mossy ground.

Rutu leapt down, turning a flip, and spoke, laughing, "And there, old man, there, is my revenge! Keep me captive, trick me, belittle me? There is your reward!"

A shadow fell across the pool, accompanied by an icy breeze, a cruel wind bearing with it the smell of dead leaves.

The fae danced circles around the stricken sorcerer. "And now the rider is here to claim you! Don't look so glum! You will have immortality after all, after a fashion. As you reminded me, no man had ever seen the great tree until today. Such will be your legacy, and your fame will live on!"

The sorcerer spat blood as he spoke, "Doubly so. My name will be known for another event."

Rutu paused his dancing. "And what is that?"

"The destruction of the great tree. Upon my life's end the fire demon contained within the ruby will win free. I need not elaborate on what will happen next. Goodbye, Rutu." With a last croaking laugh Malathiksos died.

In the distance Rutu heard a detonation followed by screaming. He scaled an oak, coming to sit in the top branches. From there he could see the great tree, completely enveloped in smoke and flame. The apprentices were rushing back to its base. Those at the fore were hurling spells at a creature comprised of flickering yellow and red. The thing coiled around the tree, writhing, hissing. From its fanged mouth came over and over, "Malathiksos! Malathiksos!"

Rutu rested his pointed chin on hand as he watched the chaos. He addressed a squirrel who sat a few feet away.

"Can you name anything, anything at all, in this universe worse than sorcerers?"

The squirrel watched, uncomprehending. Reflections of the distant flames danced across the oil black of its eyes.

# The Saga of Adalwolf

"Fear is the heat of the forge, the beating of the hammer. If the iron is good then a good blade may come of it. If the iron is poor then something brittle and useless will be born and broken soon after. When you face men across the field of battle, then we will see what kind of iron you are made of. You have my blood in you. Trust in it, and bring no shame upon our tribe. And be wary. Victory will test your iron in ways defeat cannot. Remember your brothers, your kin, your fealty to the gods."

Adalwolf always recalled his father's advice before a battle, as he did now, standing with his warlord's host and waiting for the bloodshed to commence. Across a field fragrant with wildflowers were arrayed the blood enemies of his tribe. The two sides hurled insults at one another as their hatred and lust for battle rose to a frothy boil.

Thankarat shouted above the din. "Brother, how many will you kill?"

His easy confidence was contagious. Adalwolf smiled and shouted back, "As many that come before my blade!"

Thankarat laughed, broad grin peeking from underneath his bushy blonde beard. He threw his arm around Adalwolf's shoulders and pulled him close. The two were much alike, tall, broad, and fair.

"Adalwolf. Take care to come out alive. We and Gasto are all that is left of our father's sons."

Adalwolf smiled. "You need not fear for me, brother. Half a dozen times I have fought alongside our warlord against his enemies. He won't say it out loud but I am a better warrior than his sons, better than anyone else of the house."

Thankarat nodded and continued, "Indeed, though it pains me to say it, you are a better fighter than me, though I be the oldest. But today is special. Today the gods will see us. They will see how we fight, heedless of our poor odds. They will know our cause is just. Faramund will pay for his slights. The gods will see and give us strength. Father and mother will be avenged."

Adalwolf felt a hand tugging his arm and looked to see a thin man bedecked in ragged clothes. Thongs strung with bones and feathers hung loose from his grimy neck.

"Gasto! You should push your way back to stand with the farmers. You have neither the chain nor the stomach for this sort of work. Go throw your twigs upon the ground and tell us we are assured of victory."

Gasto fidgeted, pushing aside an errant lock of dirty, dark hair and replied, "I do not come to the fore to meet the first charge. I came to show you! Look above!"

Two ravens circled overhead.

"Brother, that is no omen. They come to eat our eyes."

"You are wrong. They have followed you all morning. They circle silently, watching you."

Adalwolf twisted a fistful of Gasto's worn tunic in his gauntleted hand and pulled the shaman close. "No games, today, brother! In a short while we will either avenge father and mother or be dead! It is not the time for tricks."

"Brother, I swear on our honor! They follow you since we

left the hall! I have never seen anything like it."

Adalwolf loosened his grasp. The two stood, eyes locked. Gasto's dark eyes were eerie amidst the black ash he wore between cheek and brow. But Adalwolf saw he was sincere. The sound of a horn distracted him.

He watched his warlord and chieftain, Gerulf, doff his helmet and lay his shield on the ground.

Thankarat wondered aloud. "A parlay? Why does he even bother? Faramund will demand all! He will ask us all to wear the collar. He has the advantage. He has no reason to seek an agreement."

Gerulf walked on long strides down the gentle slope, gray hair whipping in the autumn breeze. The torrent of taunts and insults ebbed as the two warlords met in the middle of the field.

The two leaders talked. From the distance only Gerulf's laugh could be heard, a sound laden with contempt rather than mirth. His weathered features were twisted in a mask of hate as he returned to the ranks. He wore again his helm and took up his oval shield, decorated with looping swirls in the shape of a crouching wolf, matching the engraved plates which hung from his helm. The wind stirred, teasing the long plume of black horse hair which adorned the crest. He addressed his men.

"Many long years we have waited for Faramund to answer for the burning of my brother's hall! The man goes south, he goes east, he goes to trade, thinking more of coin than his honor! Finally he could ignore us no longer or be unmanned. So he comes today to the appointed place and at the appointed time. I gave him once last chance. I demanded a fair price for the burning of my brother's hall! He refused!"

Gerulf raised his arms as a tide of curses and fell oaths

washed over him. His men screamed for blood. He called for silence.

"Insult was then heaped upon insult! He demands we pay him fealty to avoid battle today! The gods know our cause is just! Faramund may buy all the blades his wealth affords, but we will win! We will have our vengeance. We of the Black Oak are the descendants of the War God. Faramund is no more than a merchant wearing a sword belt! We will kill his men and hang their corpses! Their blood will soak the sacred groves! Their screams will echo from mountain to mountain! Faramund the fat! Faramund the pig! We will gut him and quarter him and feed the meat to our hounds! So I swear before all the gods!"

Gerulf drew his blade and started down the slope, surrounded by his sons and underneath his wolf banner. Adalwolf and Thankarat rushed to get level with their chieftain. Gasto fell behind, muscled aside by larger men. Adalwolf spared one look upwards. Two ravens still circled above.

His foes approached. The hosts neared each other and men gave themselves completely over to madness and hate, breaking into a run, eager to come to blows.

The scream came unbidden to Adalwolf's throat. He felt at once weak and strong as cold sweat soaked the wool underneath his coat of chain. His stomach roiled even as a peculiar giddiness assailed a mind nearly mad with fear and rage. Through a red haze he marked the man opposite in the approaching line of foes. He was a tall man, red beard spilling from under the plates of his spagenhelm.

*All-Father, watch, witness me kill this man.*

## The Saga of Adalwolf

Red Beard aimed a powerful swing of his axe at Adalwolf but his strike was ruined by an inadvertent bump. Adalwolf parried the spoiled blow with ease and thrust savagely. The man reeled back and Adalwolf fell forward, loathe to release his grip on the sword. A blow glanced off his helm as he fell. He looked up to see Thankarat bury his axe in his assailant's shoulder. He stood and placed his boot on the bearded man's chest and pulled his blade free from where it had stuck amidst bones of the face and skull. Adalwolf brought his shield up to parry another blow, answering with a wild strike that took the man's hand off at the wrist. A blow he did not see shattered his shield. He reeled then threw himself forward, ducking a swing from a mustachioed easterner, one of Faramund's mercenaries. He feinted a thrust upwards but sliced downward instead, opening a long gash in the man's unarmored leg. Adalwolf stood fully and aimed a killing blow that found only air as the man lost his footing. The fair warrior screamed in frustration at the chaos of the melee. A blade cut into his shoulder and he spun wildly, raking his blade across the face of his attacker.

The madness came fully now. Chest heaving, howls of rage and grief burning his throat, he spun and hacked, an arm off here, a leg above the knee there, a head. The loss of his shield meant he dare not stay still. Blades found him, cutting his arms and testing the armor on his back. But all who touched him fell under his sword. There was a roaring in his ears, the sound that had haunted his sleep now for many years. It was the roar of timbers aflame, his father's hall burning, the screams of his mother and sisters, nearly drowned out by that terrible roar. The woeful cacophony lent strength to his limbs as he lay waste to his foes. Faramund's men, the mercenaries, the pitiable farmer who found himself thrust into the center of the melee, all fell, screaming except when Adalwolf's blade separated head from shoulders. He had no thought for the battle around him, not for victory or defeat. There was nothing but death, the bitter wine of vengeance that warms the blood even as it chills the soul.

Then he fell.

Legs suddenly tangled, he tumbled backwards. His sword lay under him so he pulled his saex from its sheath and raised it to strike as he lay in the blood soaked ground.

"Brother, no!"

He saw Gasto, blood stained and muddy, thin arms wrapped around his legs.

"Release me!"

Gasto did as ordered and the pair stood. The shaman pulled at his arm now. His voice was nearly a shriek as he implored, "Brother the battle is lost. Only a dozen of us remain!"

"Then I die. So be it. I have killed many men." The world around Adalwolf began to spin.

"You bleed from a half dozen wounds! Look around you! All our cousins and friends lay dead!"

"What makes you think we are not to join them?"

"Fool! What else do you see?"

Adalwolf squinted his eyes. He could see a ground littered with corpses and crying wounded. He could hear the clang of steel against steel and the throaty yells of hateful joy, the exultation of victory. But he could see little beyond a dozen feet.

"Fog..."

"Yes, brother! Sent by the gods! Clearly we are meant to escape!"

Adalwolf's vision narrowed to a small cone ringed with

gray haze. He felt himself running, pulled along by the tireless Gasto. The noise of the battle receded as they fled.

The field was gone suddenly, replaced by thick woods. Gasto led Adalwolf to a stream and guided him to sit. Handfuls of icy water brought sense back to the warrior.

"Thankarat..."

Gasto replied, eyes downcast. "Fallen."

Adalwolf closed his eyes a moment. Images of his brother leapt unbidden from the corners of his mind like startled pheasant.

The shaman sensed his brother's thoughts. "Come back to the present, brother."

Adalwolf nodded. His voice was barely above a whisper as he spoke, "We lost."

"We did. Now you must steel yourself. We must fly to the hall. Faramund's men will be looting the field for a long while. Then they will go to Gerulf's hall to claim their spoils proper. We must beat them there and take Sigga and your son and flee."

"We lost. Faramund lives."

Gasto pulled off Adalwolf's helm and filled it with water and tossed the contents across his brother's face.

"Enough!"

Thoughts of his wife and child gave speed to Adalwolf's steps. Though none were serious the warrior was weak from his wounds. But he dare not slow his pace and risk arriving too late. The pair followed the stream until it intersected with a woodcutter's path which led directly to the village. Dusk was at their backs when they finally reached the hall. Everywhere in the village women and children idled apprehensively. Gasto's news of the battle struck like lightning. Women grabbed bundles packed the night before, done in secret so as not to harm the men's morale. With children in tow they fled for the sanctuary of friendly houses in other villages. Some sat with resignation. Most wept. All looked at Adalwolf with hostility. He reddened at their unspoken accusation. Gasto sensed his shame.

"Hold your head high, brother. The gods chose you to live. They must intend you to continue to seek retribution, payment for the blood debt."

"I feel a coward."

"No! The gods preserved you. The ravens! Then the fog! Had you ever seen anything like that? Since when does fog descend when the sun is at its zenith? The gods will was clear!"

"Explain that to these women."

Adalwolf flung open the doors of Gerulf's hall with arms devoid of strength. The fire inside was low. Sigga sat in the gloom, at work on her loom next to a guttering candle. The other women of the household recoiled, walking to the rear of the hall.

Sigga was stiff in Adalwolf's embrace.

"Where is Radulf?"

"Behind you."

The boy cut a sad figure, wooden sword in hand but tears streaking his soft face. Adalwolf knelt before him and held the boy's head in his gauntleted, blood stained hands.

"Grab your clothes, boy. And help your mother gather food and blankets." He turned back to Sigga. "Have Marcus saddle our horses." She stared at him a moment before looking away.

Adalwolf felt his blood rise. "Make haste, woman!

Faramund's men will be here before the moon's rise!"

"I am not leaving."

"You are not leaving? What madness is this? Faramund will make you a slave! He will give you to his outlanders for sport and tether Radulf to a plow!"

"He won't."

"What are you talking about?"

"I had a message from my cousin, the one married to Alfwin, a son of Faramund. She said the warlord would grant us mercy. She said if the battle went against Gerulf that I might be given to another of Faramund's sons and thus make peace between his and my father's house."

Adalwolf felt his knees weaken and found a seat on a bench. "So, you would join the house of those that burnt my father's hall."

"I must think of myself and of Radulf."

The anger came like a physical thing, a black blood pumped from poisoned heart, filling his limbs with sudden strength. Adalwolf stood and drew his blade.

"My son? You would have my son join that house?"

"While you would make him live like a hunted animal until the inevitable. Faramund's men will find you. They will kill you slowly, as befits an outcast, and they will put a collar on Radulf and sell him south to be a catamite for some fat lord."

An inchoate cry of rage reverberated within the hall's stout timbers. Adalwolf raised his arm. Sigga stepped back, putting the loom between herself and her enraged husband.

A voice gruff with long years sounded from deep within the gloom of the hall.

"Stay your hand, son-in-law." The man stepped into the rays of ochre that streaked in from the open door, outlining a large frame stooped with age. Ice blue eyes peered at Adalwolf from atop a great gray beard. His gnarled hands held a naked blade.

Adalwolf was yet gripped by insensate rage, now focused on the old man. He grasped for words. "Gernot, father of my wife." The warrior gestured to Radulf, now clutching at his mother's skirt. "My son..."

"Stays here. Now leave at once before I show you the strength that remains in these old arms. I was splitting skulls while you suckled at your mother's tit. If what Gasto says is true then Gerulf is gone and so is his house. You are a warrior worthy of respect. But you are one man, a man who is already dead. Leave and go be an outcast if you must. But let the living continue on in whatever ways they see fit."

With a growl Adalwolf stepped forward. Gernot raised his blade and swung down. The young warrior's eyes widened, parrying only at the last moment. There was terrible clang and a sudden burning pain across Adalwolf's face. He looked down.

Not a hand's width of blade remained of his prized sword. Fresh blood dripped onto his armor where a fragment of the broken blade had sliced his cheek.

"Adalwolf! Come!"

Gasto waited at the door of the hall, gesturing madly.

He shouted again, "Adalwolf! Outlanders have crested the hill. We have not a moment to spare!"

In a daze Adalwolf walked toward his brother. He mumbled, "My wife and son will not follow me. My blade is shattered..."

Gasto pushed Adalwolf, nudging him to mount the palfrey he held by the reins. A woman from the hall darted out to spit at Gasto.

"Coward!"

He wiped the spittle from his face as he mounted another horse.

"Well! I was wondering how this day could get worse. Thank you, woman, a just punishment for my failure of imagination."

He kicked the small horse into a gallop, heading west. After a last look around Adalwolf did the same. Above the western road two ravens circled.

When the moon began to sink Gasto led them off the road. They found a clearing surrounded by towering pine and made a fire. Adalwolf stripped off his armor and tunic and washed in a nearby stream. Back at their camp Gasto had laid out a wool cloak for his brother along with a hunk of bread and dried fish.

Adalwolf stared into the fire as he ate without relish. Gasto hovered, binding his wounds with strips of linen.

"You have been a poor traveling companion today."

The warrior looked up at the shaman. "What would you have me say, brother?"

"I think you should thank me, for a start."

Adalwolf shook his head. "Thank you for what?"

"I saved your life twice today."

Adalwolf stood. The dancing firelight played across the looping tattoos that wound their way across his muscular torso, giving them a sort of life. He paced as he spoke, voice low and laden with bitterness.

"You have saved nothing. I am a warrior without a house, without even a sword. My wife betrayed me and my son will come to live in the hall of the man that killed his grandfather."

Gasto sat on a log and warmed his hands. "Well, indeed it sounds horrible when you say it like that. But, my brother, you live! While you live there is hope. The gods have singled you out."

"I curse all of them. The war god, the All-Father and his wife, I curse them all."

Gasto shot to his feet. "No! Brother! Take it back!"

"I will not."

The shaman came before his brother. He knelt down, bringing his eyes level with the warrior's. Adalwolf looked up.

His brother's eyes bored into his. They seemed to glow, drinking the moonlight as the flames' reflections played across them like a fox darting through an autumn wood. He spoke in a hushed whisper. "Take it back, brother. You do not know what you say."

"I take it back."

Gasto sat with a loud sigh, relieved.

Adalwolf pondered aloud. "Gerulf was a good man. He made the sacrifices, honored the gods. And his cause, our cause, was just."

"We do not know why they do the things they do, brother. Perhaps our warlord hid a black soul in his breast. Perhaps his house was fated to fall, or cursed long ago. We do not know."

"My heart cries out for vengeance. I can hear father's voice on the wind, imploring, wondering why Faramund yet lives. I have failed him."

Gasto wrapped himself in a thick cloak. "You have a head of stone and listen to nothing that I say. You live. As long as you live there is hope. Now, it has been a tiring day. Sleep and tomorrow the dawn will warm your heart."

Faramund finally slipped from the warrior's thoughts like the passing of a storm.

But Sigga came in its wake. Memories of her beauty flooded Adalwolf's mind, preventing sleep.

He saw her eyes, blue ringed by a band the color of wheat. She had been a good woman, a good wife and mother, an ally and a lover. She had tended his wounds, taught Radulf the names of the gods, and managed his coin lest the brash young man lose it in games of dice. He remembered his beaming pride when she accepted his offer of union. He remembered their lovemaking. Their people voiced passion with whispers in the dead of night lest they wake others in the village where lay their small house, or those in the hall when they slept under the warlord's roof. Love was spoken with a look over the shoulder, a smile, a kiss stolen while fetching water. Love was never flaunted. Thus the ever present jealousies engendered in close communities were not tempted into bloody release, a constant danger amongst a people so suited for war and so dedicated to vengeance.

But she was gone now. Soon, if not already, married into Faramund's house.

The smell of a coming storm filled Adalwolf's nose, snapping him from his bitter reverie. The warrior stood, slow and mindful of noise, turning in the direction of the storm. Gasto's snoring continued unabated.

To the west black clouds smothered the moon, sending the world into thick darkness. No rain came, nor lightning save one bolt, stark and blinding, snaking its way west in the direction of the road ahead.

Adalwolf laid down again, finding himself finally utterly exhausted with no more hatred to spend on images of his foes nor sadness for the face of his lost love.

In his dream a red serpent sprung from his hand to kill his foes. He laughed but the viper turned, poised to strike him, and then he awoke.

THe red rays of dawn turned the pines' frost into necklaces of bright amber. The pair awoke slowly, sore from their ordeal. Gasto inspected Adalwolf's wounds and pronounced them mercifully free of taint. The warrior's mood was not improved. After a short conversation the pair agreed to head south. There amidst the southerners Adalwolf could find work in their great armies, the numberless hosts of legend. They were mighty forces, yet not so mighty that they could ever cross the river into the lands of Adalwolf's people. Rumor always had it that the foreigners held the warriors of the north in high esteem and would pay good coin if one was willing to accommodate their bizarre practices.

It was a subject the well-traveled Gasto could expatiate at length. Free from the obligations of a warrior and naturally curious, the shaman had wandered years in the outlands. He spoke at a hare's pace, reminiscing and recounting as the horses walked the road.

"They eat mice there. They make their halls from stone. Men and women from a thousand places walk the streets gibbering to each other in their respective tongues. On festival days they make their slaves kill each other."

"As we do."

"No brother, the fight portends no augury. It is sport, a contest. Though it must please their war god especially well. Their armies have never been defeated save when they came north."

"Our gods are stronger."

Gasto's next comment was interrupted by a loud squawk.

The brothers looked up to see two ravens sitting atop a pine.

Gasto smiled, "Brother…

"I see. More ravens, and in a pair as before."

"It is the same pair And they laugh at us."

Adalwolf cocked his head. "I hear nothing."

"Ravens laugh with their eyes."

The two stared at the birds, transfixed until their horses reared.

Adalwolf was thrown from his mount. The warrior landed flat on his back, winded and gasping. He gathered his wits, coming to his elbow and watching his horse return the way they had come. In the distance he could hear his brother shouting as he fought to get his bolting mount back under control.

He came to his feet, a dire oath on his lips, arms raised in frustration. There was a sense of motion from the corner of his eye. He spun around, heart in mouth, startled to see a man in the road.

He was swathed in a cloak of faded gray, hood drawn low. A long beard woven in thick braids lay across his broad chest. The beard was steel gray but the man seemed young in posture, tall and straight backed. From a simple belt hung pouch and dagger.

In his hand was a spear. It was of good make but unadorned. The steel head shone bright in the sun though the man was mostly in shadow. Adalwolf peered into the hood. The man had strong features, weathered and cracked by sun and wind. The warrior stepped forward. He nodded his head and spoke.

"Well met, elder stranger. You gave me quite a start." The words seemed to die in his throat, tapering to a mere whisper at the end of his speech. The old man stepped  forward.

Adalwolf found he could not look up. He forced himself to meet the man's gaze, fighting a wordless impulse to flee.

The man inspected him a moment. Adalwolf saw a band of gray cloth hid his left eye. With no words, nor even a change of expression, the old man stepped forward. Adalwolf felt a pressure on his chest, felt it difficult to breathe.

The old man handed him the spear.

Unthinking, Adalwolf reached forward to take it. He met the man's gaze again, and nodded, thinking to say "thank you" but unable.

The spear was heavy in his hands, of a wood unlike any he had seen. The shaft was perfectly straight. Faint waves ran across the surface of its cutting edges. He stared at the weapon, spellbound. He tore his gaze away to try again to speak thanks to the man. But there was no one there.

The old man was gone.

Faramund found the warlord's chair in Gerulf's hall was too small to accommodate his bulk. He barked a command in the easterners' tongue and two of his mustachioed house guards removed it. While it commanded none of the grandeur he felt was his due, a simple bench would have to do for the evening. The celebration was just beginning. Mead was being poured and venison roasting. Faramund dulled his growing appetite with a plate of cheese and dried fish. The women and children of Gerulf's house, those that had remained, sat chastened, eyes downcast. Those of noble blood sat near him, beneath the platform, while the women of lesser birth sat at the end of the hall, fending off the advances of Faramund's men. Many wept quietly for their men that yet lay on the field, food for crows. The beaming conqueror would have none of it.

"No more weeping! This evening is a happy occasion! Yesterday I won a great battle! Now this hall and its people are under the leadership of a proper man!" He stood, arms raised in triumph, the fire's light glinting from his fine coat of chain. It was unmarked by any bite of blade, its wearer having done no actual fighting in the battle.

His bondsmen cheered. The fat man continued. "And further, we celebrate a wedding! My son Gunter will be joined with Sigga, the Jewel of the Black Oaks! Her father Gernot's house will regain its former glory, unchained now from Gerulf's yoke."

The old man smiled meekly as he raised his horn of mead toward Faramund. Fists slammed against table as the men yelled their approval. The easterners, ignorant of the language, focused their attention solely on drink. Faramund's wife, a raven haired beauty from a land far away, sat bored, fingering the embroidered hem of her blouse of red silk. Her eyes were pensive, dark, the color of fertile earth.

Faramund gestured for the bride.

"Let it be done!"

She emerged from the gloom of the back of the hall. Her face was a mask under the flower garland she wore. Gunter stood from his chair at the end of the warlord's table. He was the product of an earlier marriage, fair like his departed mother but heavyset like his father. He wore no armor, having spent the battle idling at Faramund's camp. His father called for a holy man.

Bent and stooped, the white robed man hobbled forward. In one hand he held a deer's antler, the other a sprig of holly. He paced in slow circles around the couple as Gunter leered. Sigga stood staring at the ground.

The warriors began a cheer, a phrase repeated over and over, an invocation. The simple chant called the attention of the gods to the coming union.

None heard the yelling outside the hall.

Gasto surveyed the slaughter. A dozen of Faramund's men, those set to guard the hall, lay dead.

"Gods! Look at this! Brother, you were always a good fighter, but one against a dozen?"

Adalwolf walked toward the hall. His already ragged armor was now stained deep with the blood of the slain. The spear was red with it, all the way to its grip. He chose a shield from amongst the dead, a poor thing from a poor warrior, but one that bore no emblem or motif, only a dull expanse of bare leather stretched over the pine. Properly arrayed he walked toward the hall.

"One man slew a dozen. Brother, you know what this means..."

Adalwolf turned and spoke, "I warned you on the road not to speak of it!"

Gasto wrung his hands, eyes wild. "How can we not speak of it! The All-Father lent you his spear! I should die from not speaking of it! I will simply burst!"

Adalwolf loomed over his brother. "Surely that is what happened! And surely if the world was meant to know the All-Father would have granted me the boon before the whole village. But only I was there. If we speak of it I will be labeled a madman. Warlords will come from far and near with two aims, to either prove me a liar or to take the spear for themselves. And perhaps I am mad! Mad with rage and grief. Now be silent! I go now into the hall. I will kill Faramund or be killed. It is time for things to end, one way or the other. It is known the gods are cruel. We shall see how cruel."

He flung the doors open, spilling the bright firelight and sounds of revelry into the chill night. He stepped forward.

For a moment Adalwolf was mistaken for one of Faramund's host. But soon he was recognized. Word spread like a leaping wildfire down the length of the benches. His blood soaked and ruined armor, his grim visage, and eyes scoured of all pity; all gave the warrior the appearance of one risen from the dead. Gerulf's widow sent out a wailing scream and lost consciousness. Faramund's men were frozen were they sat.

Adalwolf looked from face to face as he walked. Those formerly of Gerulf's house would not met his eyes. Nor did Sigga, seated at the warlord's bench and wearing the bride's garland.

Faramund inspected the young warrior then stood from his bench, sputtering. "Adalwolf! Bastard of Gerulf's brother! Have you come to pledge fealty and beg my favor? You have a strong arm, young man. I may be inclined to let you take a place in my host."

"No, Faramund. I come to kill you. My father's ghost cries for your blood. Come, draw steel and let justice be finally done."

The heavyset man laughed heartily. He looked askance at his men, who soon joined him in laughter, though without much conviction. The air of the hall was heavy in the lungs suddenly.

Faramund sat back on his bench. "Boy, I do not fight duels. That is sport for younger men." He patted a bulging purse at his waist. "What need have I for shows of shallow honor when it is gold that buys true loyalty? No, boy, you have come to die!'" He shouted a hoarse word in the thick tongue of his mercenaries. They tossed aside drinking horns and drew blades, smiling as they did. The celebrants crowding the benches scattered, seeking safety in the rear of the hall.

The men threw themselves at Adalwolf, climbing over table and bench, eyes glazed with drink and lust for blood. The warrior lowered his spear.

This time he heard no roaring in his ears. He heard every noise as clear as the sound of a pebble striking a still pool. He heard the sound of a drinking horn fallen to the earthen floor. He heard the wood of a table creak under the weight of a mercenary who stood atop, launching himself at Adalwolf. He heard his own breathing, measured and calm.

Then he struck. The spear came quicker than any could imagine, darting through the melee like a striking serpent, turning, swinging. The man leaping from the table was impaled the nearly length of it, expelling his last ale tinged breath into the face of his killer. The death gave his compatriots pause. Adalwolf kicked the body free and brought the gore stained head to bear on its next victim, leaving the man's neck a red ruin. They came from his right and left, from behind, some meeting the iron tipped end of the spear, the others meeting its lethal head. In Adalwolf's hands it was a scythe, cutting down his enemies like so many stalks of wheat. From the corner of his eye he spied Faramund attempting escape. White hot rage filled his breast. He leapt to intercept the man.

A hand grasped at his plated boots with a grip of iron, causing him to stumble. The mercenary grinned through a mouth full of blood. The man was disemboweled but not yet dead, and now drew a dagger to dispatch Adalwolf.

Across the hall Gunter found courage at the sight of Adalwolf on the ground. He stood, taking a sword from the floor and ran to where the warrior lay. More of Faramund's men saw the opportunity, the spell of Adalwolf's red dance broken.

Adalwolf kicked savagely at the one who held his leg, caving in the forehead. He tried to bring the spear to bear, difficult from where he lay. His foes closed. A blade found his shoulder. The spear was kicked from his grip. He got to his knees, lashing out with his shield's edge, rewarded by a rain of shattered teeth. Another blade gouged at his back. His half drunk assailants crowded in on each other in their eagerness, spoiling each other's strikes. Adalwolf struck out again and again, desperate for space, desperate for time. He looked frantically for his weapon.

A cut on his leg brought him back to his knees. He threw himself down, rolling, under a table now.

There it was.

He grasped the weapon and struck upward with the but, splitting the table in half. He leapt upward through the debris, thrusting, lashing. His foes fell screaming. Again and again he stabbed and swung. Footing became difficult as the ground was soon covered with the dead and dying, tables overturned, benches flipped. He realized now he struck at their backs; they were fleeing. The press of men jammed the door. They were killed like rats trapped in a granary, panicked and scurrying, eyes wide with animal terror. Gunter died impaled, writhing like an injured animal, grasping ineptly at the blood slick shaft.

The red veil fell from his eyes and Adalwolf saw men kneeling, raising their hands, yielding before him. The warrior stood atop a pile of bodies. He was a thing from the realm of the dead, horrible in the firelight, blood stained and chest heaving. The hall was silent except for the groans of the dying. The women had no more screams left. Those of the men not wounded stood crowded against the wall in terror.

Adalwolf looked around the hall, peering underneath table and bench.

Gasto was at his side suddenly, marveling at the carnage.

"Well, there's an evening's work."

"Faramund is gone."

People still stood dumb, a pitiable group, those that remained of Gerulf's house and what was left of Faramund's host. Among them there were a half dozen easterners untouched. They had sat out the fight, first trusting others to slay Adalwolf, then watching in shock as the fair warrior had laid so many low. They spoke to each other in hushed whispers. Finally one stepped forward and addressed Adalwolf. The young warrior shook his head, knowing not a word of their tongue.

From the darkness of the back of the hall she stepped forward, Faramund's wife. Her hair lay like black silk over shoulders draped with fine pelts. She spoke, voice dusky and thickly accented.

"I know their speech. They offer loyalty. They have never seen any fight as you. They ask coin to seal offer. It is their way."

Adalwolf let his shield fall. With his free arm he grabbed her waist, feeling roughly, eliciting a muffled cry. He tore a pouch of coin from her jeweled belt and tossed it to the easterner.

"Tell him I accept his bond."

She relayed the message. Adalwolf stepped onto the platform and seated himself on the place of honor.

He spoke, "I am now lord here."

Gasto leapt atop a table and affected a swagger as he paced back and forth, addressing the assembled.

"Did you hear that? My brother is now lord here. He assumes all lands and loyalties once owed Gerulf, his uncle, won by force of arms. So the gods witnessed. So was their apparent will."

The announcement broke the dark spell, the lingering horror of the slaughter all had witnessed. Suddenly there was talk. Adalwolf barked an order and slaves began to drag the corpses from the hall.

The women of Gerulf's household came forward. Uncertainty now gave way to ritual. Loyalties, however quickly they might change, must be witnessed, displayed for all and the gods to see.

Ima, Gerulf's widow, stepped forward first. She held Radulf's little hand in hers. She bowed before Adalwolf. The warrior nodded in reply and the woman stepped to take her place on the platform as a woman of high birth. She pulled the boy to her lap, whispering comfort as he buried his face in her neck.

The act was repeated, by aunts and grandmothers, and the finally the men, those of Gerulf's house that were not fighters, too old or crippled.

Then Sigga. She stepped forward but was stayed by Adalwolf's hand. She would not meet his eyes as he spoke.

"Be gone from my sight. The bond which you broke will remain so."

She left without plea or protest. Gernot followed.

Then there were Faramund's men. Of those that had been in the hall a dozen and a half remained alive. Another few were wounded, perhaps mortally. The able bodied stood completely cowed, in awe of Adalwolf, having witnessed him, one man, kill nearly fifty. Adalwolf addressed them.

"Which of you would join my host?"

Six of the men stepped forward. The rest stood defiant.

Adalwolf beckoned the raven woman forward. She stepped forward, a scowl marring her beauty.

"Tell the sell swords to bind these six men. We shall spill their blood at the feet of the oak to give thanks for my victory." He turned to the defiant ones. "The rest of you may go. When you find your lord tell him that I am coming. Tell him his wife is now my bed-slave. Tell him his son's corpse will hang from the sacred oak. He may rally more men and met me at a time and place. Or he can wait until I find him. It matters not. Go."

The men wasted no time in leaving.

By torchlight the sacrifices were made. Life's blood soaked the ground as Gasto danced and the people watched, singing a droning hymn up toward the bright stars. The slaves threw ropes over the low branches and pulled, raising up a score of bodies, hung by their feet. The rest were decapitated and their heads were piled against the trunk. The warlord was pleased at the efforts. The raven haired woman stood at his side.

Adalwolf spent the days that followed in leisure. He submitted to the attentions of Faramund's former wife who had identified herself as Phaidyme. She dressed his wounds and brought food to his great bed in the hall's loft as he idled, brooding.

In her halting speech she had relayed the story of her life to Adalwolf. After an unremarkable childhood she had been taken into the house of a powerful lord, a rich man who claimed dozens of wives in the manner of some lords of far nations. Her low birth left her without protection against the venomous envy of another wife. Her enemy poisoned the lord's ear with false rumors. Enraged, her master sold her to a merchant from the north. She found herself in a land of cruel cold under the rule of cruel gods. Her beauty commanded a great sum from Faramund, so impressed that he called her his wife, a jewel so precious it must be near him at all times and on display for all. She had been watched over constantly by Faramund's mercenary bodyguard. For all their savage tempers the swarthy men had recognized her as a fellow outlander among the blue-eyed people in their land of dark forests and rolling hills. They had taken pity on her and treated her as they would a daughter. Were it not for Faramund's odious attentions her time in the north would have been more or less bearable. But a dull ache was ever present in her heart. She could never return home, having no more family or place there, nor having any idea how to find it.

Adalwolf told her of his life. His father had been brother to Gerulf, a great warlord and just chieftain, loved by his people. His father had once given shelter to a man fleeing Faramund's rage and the fat man took it as grave insult. The two men had made peace one Yule and all was thought forgotten but Faramund had only done so to put Adalwolf's father at ease.

Gasto was touched by spirits and as a boy would often be by seized by short bouts of madness. On the evening of the burning the wolves in the forest were howling like none had ever heard before. Gasto was stricken. He leapt from table to bench, howling in return, finally darting out the door.

Thankarat and Adalwolf ran to find him.

The three returned to witness the burning. They hid under pine boughs as the screams echoed throughout the valley. They fled to Gerulf's hall where the kind warlord raised them alongside his own children. After that day Adalwolf had spent every waking moment preparing for war. He never again played a child's game. He grew into a powerful man, skilled with blade, fair features perpetually dark with the burden of a blood debt. Gerulf dutifully sought battle with his brother's murderer, persisting after Faramund's many absences and evasions and the passage of long years. But when finally granted their wish for battle their house could not summon the numbers needed to match those bought by Faramund's great coffers.

Adalwolf did not tell her of the spear.

They spoke deep into the night. When all had been said Phaidyme gave to Adalwolf what he had declined to take by force. They lay until awake for a long while afterwards. Adalwolf marveled at the beauty of her strange complexion, warm amber in the light of an oil lamp, while Phaidyme traced his many scars and tattoos with her delicate fingers, aghast at his paleness and in awe of his strength.

Visitors came with the dawn. Adalwolf received them as he broke his fast with a meal of mutton and bread. They were three brothers, introducing themselves as Hartmut, Leudagar, and Odalric, landless young men from a village north. They were of a kind, ruddy faces and reddish hair worn in a knot, stout of build yet not as tall as the fair warrior who they approached. They wore no chain but each carried a broad axe, a two handed weapon more suited to cleaving men than wood. They stepped before the platform.

Adalwolf spoke his name.

Hartmut, the eldest, spoke, "It must be you, then, lord. Two days ago a man came to our village. He had left many years ago to make a name for himself as a warrior and came to serve in the house of Faramund. This man spoke of a warrior named Adalwolf that had slain a host single-handed. The fell warrior spared him and bade him warn his lord but the man had no more stomach for war and thus made his way to the village of his birth to work another's land and live in peace. You must be the fell one, Adalwolf, slayer of fifty men."

Gasto cocked his head, "More like forty or forty five methinks.

Adalwolf ignored him. He replied to the three, "Aye, I slayed many men."

The three bowed. "Let us join your warband. We swear on our father's honor to serve you faithfully. Let us go to war with you and share in your glory."

"I accept your bond. But know at the moment we boast few spears."

Hartmut smiled. "It is good. We shall be marked as one of the first."

They made their vow and Adalwolf embraced them.

More came over the winter that followed. From villages far and near they came to fight alongside Adalwolf the slayer, Adalwolf the Indomitable, Cheater of Death and Sower of Grief.

Many were young men, unproven. But others were older, hard men. Some had served in the southern hosts and still wore their hair short in the way of the southerners. Adalwolf named a new hearth guard for himself. Hartmut and his two brothers were put at places of honor as was Othmar and

Radobod, veterans of the south, cunning men and well experienced in war. Othmar was a wiry man, balding and gray at the temples but yet boasting the strength of younger men. Radobod was his opposite, thick as a mighty oak. He still carried his blade from the south, a short weapon but broad and heavy, seeming all the shorter when wielded by his great arm. Both spun tales of fighting across the southern empire, in the fertile west where men decorated themselves with woad and far away to the east in lands with no trees and a pitiless sun

The easterners were always near, watching all with eyes like the hawks which soared over the steppes of their far home. Phaidyme sat at his side always and Gasto next to her.

Soon the warlord led a host that rivaled that of Faramund on the day of the battle lost. Winter gave way to spring and on the feast of Oestre Adalwolf ordered the sacrifices made and announced the host would soon march against Faramund. The news was expected, days earlier he had sent out messengers to carry his challenge to Faramund. He made the messengers repeat his words over and over so that they not forget.

Adalwolf, Lord of the Black Oaks, beseeches Faramund come with the men of his house to meet on the field and answer for his crime. If he chooses not to fight on the field then Lord Adalwolf will come into his lands and his villages. He will raze all before him and leave nothing larger than a mouse alive.

At night they feasted in the hall. Faramund's messenger arrived, a hulking man wearing fine furs and bearing a shield painted with his lord's chosen emblem, a boar rendered crudely. The herald brought news that his lord agreed to meet at the appointed time and place. The man was given food and drink and allowed to return unharmed as per ancient tradition even as the very sight of a man under Faramund's bond made Adalwolf's blood rise. He gripped the spear tight, fighting the urge to cut the messenger down where he sat.

Gasto stood atop table and bench, telling the story of their father's death and the blood debt that yet haunted them. The shaman spoke of the treachery and cowardice of Faramund, how his brother had challenged an entire warband and slain them all, forty men in one night, here on the very floor on which they slept. The shaman flung his body here and there for effect, eyes wide and arms gesticulating madly. An old man's walking stick served as the spear, the weapon that had laid so many low on that bloody night. Adalwolf used to bristle at the tale's telling but he found it now gave him pleasure to hear.

The ale flowed, the fires burned, and the warlord's rage became their rage, his blood debt became theirs. In the throes of drink warriors stood before Adalwolf and pledged dire oaths, that they would kill six men or spill their own blood onto the sacred oak, that they would be the first to draw blood in the battle, that they would wear no chain or helm for the fight, many such oaths.

Phaidyme shook her head, speaking to no one in particular, "Surely there are none more mad than these people cursed by their gods to live as wolves."

The fires burned low as one by one the men dropped off to dreamless sleep. Adalwolf sat in his chair, watching the embers. In his hand he held the spear. The wood was warm in his hands, alive.

"Do you not hear me, brother?"

Adalwolf looked to his brother, perched on the platform.

"Ah, you do hear me."

Adalwolf spoke finally. "I hear you. What had you been saying?"

The shaman fingered his necklace of bones. "Oh, nothing, just wondering how many men Faramund will field."

"It matters not."

"I suppose it doesn't. No weapon is as mighty as yours. I shall have another tale to tell in a few days, another story to add to your legend."

"Fifty."

Gasto cocked his head, sending a quizzical look toward his brother. Adalwolf yet stared at the embers. "What do you mean, brother?"

"I killed fifty men. During the tale-telling you said I killed forty. It was at least fifty."

Gasto laughed, a sound cut short by a look from Adalwolf.

"If you say so, brother."

Adalwolf's host marched to the field. There waited Faramund, resplendent in shining chain and greaves of iron trimmed in gold. His host was larger than Adalwolf's by a half. He looked across the field, arms folded over his great stomach, smirking. One of his bodyguard blew a hunting horn, an invitation to discuss terms.

Adalwolf ignored the signal, offering no parlay. He turned to his men and raised his spear, loosing a battle cry which echoed from the hills. The men shouted their low battle call into the backs of their shields. The sound reverberated across the field, a sound felt as much as heard. Adalwolf turned to face his foes and the host advanced.

The two warbands crashed against each other unleashing a cacophony of clanging steel and splitting shields. In the center was Adalwolf, striking again and again with the spear. Men fell by the dozen to its point which never dulled. The field of enemies thinned before him as he cut a great swathe through their ranks.

Ahead was Faramund, fleeing. What remained of his host had completely broken, resolve shattered by the spectacle of death at the fore, death wielding a spear as fast as a viper. Adalwolf was the embodiment of the world as it was, death without mercy, life without salvation, a world where one survived only by depriving another of life. Vengeance and greed, hunger and darkness, a world where with few exceptions only women grew old, and not many at that. Death and life, one inevitable as a mountain and the other as fleeting as a song on the wind. There justice came only at the point of a spear and peace was a madman's dream.

As the fat man's host ran pell-mell from the field Adalwolf's men became as wolves running down deer, exulting in the chase. Fleeing men were set upon with savage glee. Spears found backs and blades rose and fell, hewing limbs and splitting skulls.

Adalwolf screamed that none should touch Faramund. His arm went back and the spear flew high, piercing the heavy-set man and pinning him to the ground where he stood. Adalwolf sprinted, coming before his enemy, desperate to see his face before the ghost left.

Faramund could not speak, his lung pierced, but looked at his killer with eyes wide with fear and hatred. Adalwolf drew his sword and took Faramund's head.

On the crest of a low hill he stood and held the bloody

thing high, displaying his terrible trophy to gods and men, bellowing in savage joy until his throat threatened to split.

His father and mother were avenged.

Around him his men looted the corpses and dispatched the wounded with a cruelty believed to be pleasing to the war god.

All stood in awe at the size of Faramund's hall. Adalwolf went through its chambers one by one, his bodyguard in tow.

"Each is like a house unto itself."

Gasto ran his hands over the timbered mantles and jambs. "The gods are skillfully rendered here. The carver must be a proud man."

Kolkoi, the leader of Adalwolf's easterners, tapped his lord on the shoulder, beckoning. The warrior and his brother traded looks. Gasto shrugged and they both followed.

Underneath a layer of straw and packed earth lay Faramund's treasure hoard.

"Gods! I have never seen so much gold!" Gasto threw up his arms in wonder.

Kolkoi grinned, an expression ruined by the scar which ran from the top of his shaved head to chin. Adalwolf rewarded him on the spot with a heavy gold ring, slipping the circle around the man's thick arm.

Gasto laughed, "Brother, you should have been a trader!"

Hartmut spat at his feet. "My lord is no trader. He is the greatest warrior to have ever lived."

Adalwolf smiled, "Brother, think. Though I am no trader is not this gold mine now?"

"I see your point."

The warrior knelt before the hoard. He thrust his hands

into the pile of coin, feeling, taking great handfuls and watching it slip from his fingers.

Gasto asked, "How much will you give to the gods? A third, I should think, no?"

Adalwolf was silent. He held a ruby up to the firelight. The flames danced in its heart of frozen blood.

"Brother?"

He turned, smiling. "I think none. My men deserve this. We shall keep half for our purposes, and half for the men. Let me be known as a ring giver!"

Hartmut and his brothers sent up a great shout. "Lord Adalwolf Ring Giver!"

Gasto fingered the bones strung along his necklace, "Brother, perhaps you should reconsider..."

"You question our lord?"

Adalwolf motioned for Hartmut to stay his hand. The young warrior took his hand from the hilt of his sword.

Phaidyme took Ima along with her sisters to Faramund's great room and kicked open the chest which contained the jewelry with which she was once adorned for his pleasure. She took up handfuls of the stuff, beautiful rings of emerald and sapphire, necklaces of gold adorned with topaz and amber, and threw them about. Laughing the women scooped up the treasures, decorating each other, a game to see who could place more on who. The raven woman's face became suddenly grim as she regarded the great bed, a thick mattress under the watch of carved dragon's heads.

Ima asked, "What troubles you, sister?"

"There is where the fat man forced himself on me."

"Well, there is only one thing for that." She called for slaves who broke the thing down and carried it outside with some difficulty.

They danced around it as it burned, hands joined and laughing, burdened by heavy gold chain and an overabundance of precious stones.

Faramund's stores contained many delicacies, among them dozens and dozens of amphorae filled with the wines of the south.

Adalwolf sat at the place of honor, quaffing the dark liquid from a goblet of bright gold. He spoke to Hartmut at his side.

"One could get used to this."

"Indeed, lord. And so should you. We should march south next."

Othmar voiced his opinion, "Nay, lord. We should march east and west. All who speak our tongue should be ruled by one. You should become a king. There has not been one since long ago when my grandfather was but a child. Then, my lord, then we march south."

Radobod added, "I marched with the southern legions in their wars in the east. They paid in good coin, seeming to have no end of it. Othmar is right. When all the tribes make war under one banner, then and only then will we have the strength to move south. A king is what is needed."

Adalwolf stared at the goblet, turning it in his hands, pondering the gems worked into the rim. In his other hand he held the spear. He spoke one word, "King..."

Hartmut shouted, "Yes! Othmar is right! King Adalwolf!"

The chant was taken up by the whole hall, save Gasto.

The next day those of Adalwolf's host who worked the land returned to their farmsteads in order to help with the coming planting. They were laden with gifts from their lord and instructed to return in the fall. Adalwolf was lavish with his coin, guaranteeing that they would return with additional men. When all had departed the warrior left the hall and its thick air to chop wood while Odalric arranged for the men that remained to fight a mock battle. Hartmut and Radobod went with their lord to the forest's edge. Gasto followed, singing quietly to himself a song of a goddess who wept tears of gold.

The day was fair and warm and the men enjoyed the luxury of working stripped to the waist. Their falling axes beat an irregular tattoo, a back drop for their boasts and jokes and easy laughter. They exchanged tales, witnessed or heard, of dire battle or witless escapade. Othmar and Radobod told them of life in the great southern host and its odd ways where the numberless men of their army men all woke at once, all ate at once, all slept at once.

"Did you all piss at once?"

Radobod shook his head no. "No, my lord, but I believe they would have asked that of us if they believed it possible."

Adalwolf asked, "And how do they fight?"

"They fight without passion." Othmar paused, reconsidering his words. "Perhaps it is more complicated. The soldiers feel the rage the same as us. But it is channeled, directed like a dog may push sheep. Their warlords insist none may move without a command. They stay in perfect lines, shield to shield, and thus protect each other. I have seen the Gaals attack, a great throng of men that crashes against their line like a wave upon the rocks. When the force is spent, the water dissipated, there the rock still stands."

"How can one beat them?"

Othmar lay his axe down and leaned against a log, brow furrowed. He replied thoughtfully, "They have lost before, no matter what rumor says. But it is difficult. If one cannot out think them, then one must overwhelm them. If you have not the force to overwhelm them, then, of course, you must out think them. That would be difficult."

Adalwolf laughed. "We must plan to overwhelm them. I'll not pit my mind against some lettered sorcerer lord from the south."

Hartmut spoke, "You must unite all underneath your banner. Only then we will have the force. Send out messengers, my lord."

"What would I tell them?"

Hartmut met his lord's eyes. "Tell them Adalwolf the Slayer beseeches all warlords to come fight with him. There is wealth undreamed in the south."

Radobod interrupted, "That is indeed true. They have more slaves than men there. They have horse carts that carry coin alone, they have so much."

"All this will be theirs if they fight with you."

Gasto shouted for silence.

"Hoofbeats! Do you fools not hear?"

The men leapt to their feet and brought axes to the ready. Adalwolf took up his spear.

A trio of horses became visible on the trail.

Ima waved and prodded young Radulf to wave too. Behind them Phaidyme rode with Alia, one of Gerulf's daughters. On the last horse was Kolkoi, at home in the saddle with blade and short bow near his hand, a cloth sack slung on his back.

Radobod struck his axe into a log, laughing. Adalwolf took Phaidyme from the saddle, holding her aloft for a moment. She yelled at the precariousness of her position and the warrior lowered her down into an embrace. Kolkoi threw down the sack but remained mounted.

Ima spread out a cloak and beckoned Radobod to sit, as did Alia and Hartmut. Phaidyme undid the lashing on the bag and produced bread, cheese, and skins of wine which Radulf passed around.

Adalwolf's laughter filled the clearing. "Gasto infected us with his fear! We thought attack was imminent."

The shaman sniffed, standing with arms folded until Phaidyme beckoned him to sit.

"There now, brother. Look at her, that smile could melt ice. No heart can be clouded in her presence."

"Indeed not, brother."

Radulf held a piece of cheese up to his uncle. Gasto bit at it and made to bite the boy's hand. The child laughed and fled, Gasto impersonating a bear as he chased him. Adalwolf took a great swig of wine and pulled Phaidyme close for a short kiss. She blushed, beating her small fist against his broad chest.

A shadow passed, Kolkoi still on his horse, making a circle around the area.

"Why does he not join us?"

Phaidyme frowned. "He speaks of dark dreams of late, a black viper hunting in tall grass, a white eagle falling."

Adalwolf saw the sunlight pouring over the tops of the trees, shining upon Phaidyme's black hair like gold dust. Sparrows' songs floated through air scented with wildflower and the smell of green wood.

"Nonsense."

Come the end of summer Adalwolf and his host lent their backs to the work of the harvest. The easy days of idling, feasting, and mock fighting gave way to endless discussion and speculation. Many warlords had agreed to meet with

Adalwolf and discuss his ambitions. Day after day more of Adalwolf's men, the ones from far villages, returned. They were impatient for news and eager for war, the way to wealth and glory.

Othmar began to fret. "We have had much interest. But nothing yet from far north, the lands of Wigmar. All know he boasts the most spears of any man that speaks our tongue. I would take him above all the others combined. They say he has three thousand men under bond."

Adalwolf wondered, "Why doesn't he march south himself? Or crown himself king?"

"He is somewhat like Faramund was, my lord. Though he is a better warrior, to be fair. He is a good fighter and a good leader but wealth is ever his goal. To attempt what you imagine, he would risk everything. We fight for you because we are warriors and you are the greatest among us. Men like Wigmar must use coin to buy loyalty."

The warlord clapped Othmar's back. "You flatter me."

"No, lord. Those who saw the slaying in your old lord's hall, they can barely speak of it."

"Gasto certainly has no problem."

"That is his gift, lord."

Hartmut scratched his short beard. "I see little of your brother lately, lord."

"He is in one of his moods. He spends most of his time in the woods of late, talking to squirrels or whatever his ilk are wont to do."

Phaidyme sat with Radulf and Gerta, Ima's daughter, weaving dolls of straw. The boy was distracted, watching two of his father's host battle with wooden poles. Ima pushed him toward the cluster of men.

"Go on, now. Watch from closer but be mindful not to get in anyone's way."

The boy ran off. Phaidyme sighed. "He has grown much. He will soon have no more time for us."

"He must make his way in the world of men. He will come back to us though, not us, of course, but women his own age, to woo and make a family."

"Unless he is killed."

Ima spat on the ground to ward against dark speech. "He will be strong like his father."

One of the men landed roughly as the others cheered the victor. The man raised his hands a moment then bent to help his erstwhile enemy to his feet. They drank water from a wooden bucket as they sweat in the summer's heat.

Ima watched. "He has shoulders like my Gerulf did, broad."

Phaidyme giggled, "Radobod has broad shoulders too."

"Yes, and he warms my bed well."

"Will you become joined?"

Ima shook her head. "Not likely. I am a widow with my own wealth and slaves to manage. And he keeps his hair short, like a southerner. Adalwolf has not asked you for marriage?"

The raven woman shook her head. "We share a bed and talk much. But something holds him back. Perhaps it is memories of Sigga's betrayal. I would never do something like that. I have nowhere to go even if I so chose."

"Are you with child yet?"

Phaidyme looked away. "No."

Ima shrugged. "Don't fret. If he wants more sons he can make them with any slave."

"Any other slave, you mean."

The widow put her arm around Phaidyme's shoulder. "I have seen how Adalwolf looks at you. Though he has not yet made you his equal it is clear he does not think of you as a slave."

"Still, I worry."

Ima pondered a moment. "With Gerulf I had trouble at first. The first year together we produced no child. I consulted a wise woman and she recommended a sacrifice. We could do the same for you."

"I suppose."

Another bout ended to more shouting. One of the men had taken Radulf on his shoulders so the boy could see. He raised his arms, sharing in the triumph. The group forgot their sport at the sight of visitors entering the village.

Three men rode on fine horses, tall and handsome creatures, unlike the hardy work horses common to the area. The man at the lead sat straight backed in the saddle, chin high. His helm was a finely wrought thing, boasting a full mask trimmed in gold. Long lengths of iron bound by leather thong protected his arms and lower legs while a fine tunic of chain sheathed his strong upper body. A black eagle adorned his iron rimmed shield. The men stopped their exercises to gather their weapons and approach the interlopers. Their leader doffed his helm, revealing a head of brown curls above a high boned face and dark beard.

"I am Siward, son of Wigmar, come to see your lord."

Adalwolf received his visitor with a proper feast. Siward accepted the hospitality with the rough grace taken for good manners among the people of the north. The warlord made him a gift of a fine saex with gold hilt. Siward handed over a tightly bound leather packet containing a rare purple dye made near his home. Adalwolf raised his eyebrows at the choice of gift.

Othmar spoke in his ear, "It is a signal, my lord. Purple is the color of the great emperors of the south."

"Oh. A positive sign, I should think."

Siward leaned forward. "My father is indeed hopeful. The riches of the south are the stuff of legend. If one could unite all the warlords and march south then we would be wealthy beyond dreams."

Hartmut leaned forward, "If I may ask, brother from the north, are you empowered to act in your father's name or are you here to merely to gather information?"

Siward ignored the question. "Who is she?" The nobleman pointed to Phaidyme. She sat sharing a cup of wine with Ima and Alia.

Adalwolf spoke, "That is Phaidyme. She shares my bed."

"I should hope so. She is the most beautiful woman I have ever seen. It is fitting she lie with a great lord. Is she your wife?"

"No."

"Where is she from?"

Adalwolf frowned. "No one knows."

Siward scratched his short beard, carefully trimmed to frame his strong jaw advantageously. He turned to Hartmut, "I am sorry. What was it you asked?"

Hartmut repeated the question.

"Ah, yes. My beloved father has empowered me to make decisions regarding the disposition of his men. The old man complains constantly of sore back and creaking joints. He won't be joining us. But I am his eldest and most favored. I have proven my mettle in a half dozen fights and he grooms me as successor though my uncles hunger for power. He has worked hard these long years to gather a host to rival any in the land. It is his wish that his son make good use of it. So, yes. I am able to make decisions."

Adalwolf, Othmar, and Hartmut traded looks.

Adalwolf asked, "Under what terms would you consent to fight under my banner, with me as crowned king in the manner of other nations?"

Siward shook his head. "I do not know. I feel I have much to learn about you as a man. Tell me about the stories I have heard. A traveler stayed in our hall a few months ago, speaking of a man who slew sixty men single handed. A man named Adalwolf."

Adalwolf smiled. "It is true. I demanded a duel with Faramund, a warlord who burnt my father's hall when I was a boy. The man set his warband on me and I slaughtered most, the others yielding."

"Impressive."

Adalwolf smiled. "My brother makes a good telling of it. Where is he? Gasto!"

The shaman was not in the hall. Adalwolf ordered his brother found. In the meantime the men drank and prodded Siward into descriptions of his father's land. They lived along the coast in a fog ridden land blessed with a good harbor. Traders from the far north brought pelts and amber there to bargain with adventurous southern merchants, making a long and dangerous trek to secure the beautiful sable and ermine always in demand in their faraway home. They brought slaves and coin aplenty, enough that Wigmar could amass a fortune as middleman and supplier of goods to sustain them on their trip back. His host ensured the merchants' safety until back over the river, no small distance.

A slave interrupted, "My lord, your brother sits in the pines north and refuses to come to the hall unless you speak with him."

Adalwolf growled. He turned to Siward, "Are any of your brothers mad?"

"Actually, no. They are all dead."

The evening was still young as Adalwolf left to find his brother. Othmar followed. The men carried torches though the moon was bright, coating the world underneath with a dust of faint luminescent silver. The noise of revelry receded behind them. The villagers' houses were open, enjoying the last few nights of warmth before autumn's arrival. Laughter was heard, children playing, women singing.

"Your people are enjoying the peace, my lord."

Adalwolf smiled. "If all unite under my banner then there will be no more war here, no more raids or burnings. All our energies, our bloodlust and greed, all will be pointed south."

"Better there than against those that speak our tongue and know our gods. And besides, the south is far richer."

The houses gave way to fields heavy with the scent of the harvest, cut wheat and decaying chaff. Beyond them was a stand of pine. The grove was thin and the ground wet underfoot. Adalwolf cursed as his boot sank into mire.

"Trust my brother to hide in a bog."

"I am not hiding, brother."

Adalwolf spun, looking.

The torchlight found him, sitting on the upturned trunk of a fallen tree, his back against the roots.

"There you are. I have come as you asked. Now come back to the hall and cause me no more shame. I was speaking with the son of Wigmar, the mighty warlord from the north. We cannot hope to march south without his spears. And now he thinks me weak, at the beck and call of my mad brother. Come now, before I lose my temper."

"We must speak, alone."

"Brother…"

"On the soul of our father! Give me a few moments at least! Mighty Adalwolf!"

Adalwolf cursed in anger and then turned to Othmar, "Wait for me at the edge of the village."

"My lord, while your campaign is merely the seed of an idea word spreads quickly. The warlords south may have caught wind of it already. Traders have passed through, the men may have boasted, it is not impossible. And it is not unheard of for the southerners to act dishonorably to destroy a threat before it becomes too dire. Lone murderers may stalk you this very moment. It is unwise for you to ever be alone."

Adalwolf raised his hands in frustration, "Is there one man under my bond or in my family that might obey me? Othmar, your concern is appreciated. Now go wait for me."

Othmar obeyed, leaving the two brothers alone.

"Speak quickly, Siward awaits."

Gasto stood and began pacing. "You know what troubles me."

"As a matter of fact, no. And I may never know if my patience grows thinner and I sink you into this bog."

Gasto's eyes were large in the moonlight, two orbs floating in black.

"The spear! The spear, you fool!"

"What about it?"

"It was given to you for righting a wrong. To defeat

Faramund and repay a blood debt. It was not given to you so that you might become a king."

Adalwolf spat, "And how do you know? The All-Father chose me to wield this weapon. Me! None others were worthy, none others were chosen! Why should I not become a king in the manner of other nations? Why should I not live in a hall of stone filled with riches and innumerable slaves? This is our destiny! No longer will our people spend their lives in wasteful slaughter. We will rule!"

"That is not why you were given the spear! The gods watch over a world they cannot control. The All-Father knew our cause was just. He gave you the spear so that you could win justice for father and mother and our kin." The shaman clutched at his brother's jacket of leather tied with iron scales. "Give it back! Throw it into the bog! March south, if you must, but do so without the spear! I have seen your ruin in dreams! I hear the birds speak of it. I hear the wolves howl in mourning. All of what we have will be lost. Throw it in the bog, I beg you!"

Adalwolf made to break his brother's grip but it was strong. Gasto's eyes bored into his from mere inches away. The shaman broke his gaze to regard the spear in Adalwolf's hand. He reached out to touch it. The warrior snapped, raising his fist against his brother.

Gasto lay dazed, bleeding profusely from a broken nose. He ignored Adalwolf's hand. The shaman spat blood onto the wet ground and stood on his own.

"Go then, make your bargain with the man from the north. Follow your destiny."

Adalwolf returned to the village's edge where waited Othmar. He thought to ask what had transpired but held his tongue upon seeing his lord's grim expression, a death mask in torchlight.

The hall was loud with laughter and song as they reentered. Hartmut met them with a wide grin on his face, intercepting them before they took their place.

"I think this Siward is warming to the idea. A dozen men gave testimony, swearing on their honor that you are the mightiest warrior ever seen. You are just and fair and a good ruler with a good mind."

Othmar laughed, "A good mind? The ale flows tonight."

Adalwolf gave his sword-brother a shot to the arm. The three resumed their places at the table at the hall's head.

Siward spoke, "Lord Adalwolf, you certainly inspire great loyalty. My father would be jealous."

"I have good men. They honor me because I honor them."

The warlord's son shrugged. "I suppose. Certainly you are an honorable man, none would say otherwise. But we of the forests and hills, we sons of the All-Father, all of us, we follow strength. Men desire glory, coin..." He paused, gazing over to where the high born women, and Phaidyme, sat drinking and laughing. "...and women. And we will take whatever path is shortest to our goals. Your men see strength in you. They calculate, and know you are the best chance to their goals."

"You are right, I suppose. Though I know not how anything else matters when a man has no honor."

Siward smiled, laying a hand on Adalwolf's shoulder. "Of course, of course. I must say I am impressed. You have many men, many veterans and many in armor. With my men, my father's men, and those of all the minor warlords, I believe we may be successful."

"So you agree to fight under my banner?"

Othmar and Hartmut leaned forward. Adalwolf looked at

Siward, searching his eyes.

He spoke finally, "I will tell my father, yes. I will return with the men and the final terms, whatever my father wishes. If you agree to the terms then we shall swear oaths and I will come under your banner. When would you like to march?"

"As soon as we are assembled at the feast for Oestre we will march."

The next day Siward left, laden with gifts for his father from Adalwolf. A chill breeze followed in his wake, advertising the coming autumn. The people of the village, their lord and his warriors, all turned their attentions toward preparing for the winter. More wood was laid in and many houses were given new thatch. At nights the warriors would crowd the benches cheering mock battles, fought by each in turn to stay fit. The hall was now too small to accommodate all the warriors at once. New houses were stood up and thatched. Men from different houses were made sword brothers to purge the warband of old rivalries, old hatreds. On market days Adalwolf spent Faramund's coin on pork and ales for the men.

He turned to Othmar as they inspected a farmer's wares, "Next spring we will see victory in the south, and much pillage I hope. These warriors are eating through our hoard. I reckon we have enough to make it through the winter with full bellies, but not far beyond."

"The south will yield all of our needs." He pulled his cloak tight against the freshening wind.

Adalwolf counted coppers from his pouch. The coins were small in his fingers, each piece embossed with a likeness of the god-king who ruled the south. The warrior cursed.

"Where is Ima? I have no head for numbers. Gods'

mysteries, why skill at killing men leads me to become a trader...And where is Phaidyme? I have not seen her all afternoon."

"I believe she goes to the forest's edge to give your brother food."

Adalwolf made noise of derision, something between a growl and a snort.

The leaves celebrated their demise in rich maroon and crimson. Phaidyme sat on a tree stump, inspecting them under the diffuse light of the sun behind gray blankets. Across her sat Gasto. Between mouthfuls of bread he thanked her.

"Yes, you are welcome. I enjoy your company and I enjoy this forest. There was nothing like this near my old home. But, Gasto, won't you ever come back to the hall? Why do you feud with your brother? They say he will be king. They will crown him and then in the spring after oyster they will march south."

"Oestre, the festival of Oestre, when all the world is renewed. But I do not feud with my brother. It is not that simple. My brother is on a path which will lead to doom. I have seen it in dreams. I have heard the animals speak of it. I have told him as much. But he is blinded to wisdom by the desires of his heart."

"What is this doom?"

Gasto shook his head as he wiped crumbs from his filthy tunic. Phaidyme's heart was heavy with pity as she regarded the thin man who sat on the leaves before her. His face was more gaunt than ever, ringed with lines of worry. His wild eyes stared out from black painted pits. He looked to the sky, searching for words.

"I cannot speak of it because I know not its form." He came to sit near the woman and reached forward for her delicate hand. He continued, "The doom may touch you. Sister, if you are ever in danger, come to this place. Wait for me here. I will learn of your arrival and come and we will escape. We will go south or perhaps even try to find your far home."

"Gasto, please. Everything will be fine. Your fight with your brother colors your dreams. All will be well. Your brother loves me and I him. He would never let harm come to me."

"I hope you are right.

Phaidyme smiled at the shaman. She saw the stains streaking the front of his tunic, a dark brown in places, a dark red in others. The man smelled of earth and leaves, and blood.

"Gasto, are you hurt?"

He cocked his head, regarding her with a quizzical expression.

Phaidyme pointed to his tunic, "Blood, Gasto. There is blood on you."

He looked down. "Oh, that. No, I am fine. That is deer's blood."

"You killed a deer?"

"No sister, I did not kill it. The wolves shared with me."

Phaidyme followed his glance toward the trees. From the corner of her eye she imagined a gray shape darting away amidst the brush.

The air grew cold but the village yet swelled with the arrival of new warriors. Word of Adalwolf's ambition had spread to every hamlet and village and young men were

117

lured to his banner as moths to flame. Faramund's great hoard, though much diminished, funded more buildings and kept the men fed.

Each new arrival stood before Adalwolf and his bodyguard and told of his name and father's name, his village, and in what battles he had fought and what men he had killed. Those whose names were known were given space in the main hall and observed closely by Hartmut and Othmar, always looking for more men of proven mettle to add to those that would stand close to their warlord in battle. Soon that number swelled to six dozen men, all armored and carrying many weapons of steel. The poorest warriors had only clubs or spears of sharpened and fire hardened wood. But they were fed as well as the body guard and thus loved Adalwolf as a just man. Many men brought their wives and children. Holy men in bedraggled white robes joined the ranks, along with many boys too young to properly fight but that might be used to hurl stones or javelins at the enemy. Scattered among the ranks were men who had fought with the legions south. Some had deserted their posts to join. A few were not even of Adalwolf's people, southerners proper of a darker complexion and speaking the tongue with a halting accent. Some brought gifts for their new lord, extra weapons or slaves. Prized especially were slaves from the south, captured soldiers or merchants. Some had been in captivity for years and showed the scars of their breaking. Others bore fresh wounds were their bonds chafed. All were reckoned good gifts, especially with Yul approaching.

On the day of the Yul feast Adalwolf sat with Phaidyme at his side, and his favorite dozen warriors flanking him to left and right. The easterners stood against the back wall.

The warlord leaned to Phaidyme, "Kolkoi and his ilk seem

unable to relax."

"Indeed, he confessed earlier that he had never seen so many people in one place save for the battlefield. It makes them nervous."

The hall roared their appreciation for a juggler who was keeping aloft an assortment of objects. He added one more but walked backwards into a bench, losing his balance. Faramund's skull clattered against the floor and all sounded their disappointment.

Adalwolf clapped heartily as his men did the same.

That night in the grove of the Black Oaks sacrifices were made. Dozens of animals were killed and their blood collected in great bowls of gleaming bronze. In the light of towering bonfires young men and women smeared the blood over the tree's gnarled trunks. When the beast's meat was boiling a group of the southern slaves were brought forward. Most died quietly though some did not. To please the gods their deaths were varied. Some were beheaded. Others had their throats slit or were hung. The holy men's white robes were red with blood as they danced.

The long weeks of winter were spent half in idleness and half in the work to create an army. Othmar arranged for the men to be organized in the way of the southern hosts. It was a difficult task, explaining to the men a new way of making war. There were many skeptics. A battle was two groups of men trying to kill each other. The larger group or the more savage or skilled group would win. So it had been since the dawn of time. The veterans from the south corrected their sword-brothers, explaining what was intended.

The men would never submit to the harsh discipline of the south, Adalwolf would not even counsel an attempt at such a scheme so the warlord and his bodyguard satisfied themselves with what they had, something more than their traditional way of war yet not near the discipline of the southern hosts. Othmar rubbed his gray temples and pronounced that their numbers and savagery would carry the day.

Winter begrudgingly relinquished its hold on the land. Spring was slow to start; the air in mornings still bit at the face and hands when Oestre neared. The festival preparations were underway when Siward's column was seen cresting the hill. He and his hearth guard rode on horseback while his spears trailed behind, a long black serpent along the road. The men of that area favored dark dyes for their wool and painted their faces and bodies with black bands. Adalwolf met Siward at the palisade's gate.

The men embraced and both hosts sent up a great cheer. None had ever seen or even heard of so great a host as Adalwolf's and Siward's combined. Adalwolf cut a striking figure in Gerulf's fine helm and his chain and greaves. In his hand, as always, was the spear. Siward's armor and clothes were even finer. His collar, cloak and sleeves were lined with ermine and the scales affixed to his leather tunic were heavy iron trimmed in gold.

But Siward's bodyguard bore his standard, not yet the wolf sigil of Adalwolf. The warlords and their best warriors entered the hall and were served ale and food by all the village's slaves.

Siward was seated at Adalwolf's right hand. Othmar and Hartmut were to his left and to the left of the guest were two of his hearth. The noise in the hall allowed the two warlords to speak in privacy. The handsome northerner smiled as he looked upon his host's set features.

"You are impatient to discuss terms, I sense."

Adalwolf nodded. "Forgive my rudeness. But we have waited months. My warriors chew at the leash, eager to move on the southerners. I now have over four thousand men at my command. You bring at least three thousand, but a higher number in armor and with proper weapons. Othmar tells me the southerners can field many more but it would take them months to assemble such a host. In the meantime we can lay waste to half their country. But every day we delay moving is another day I have to feed these hungry bastards."

"As I said I would, I told my father that we should fight under your banner. So we are here."

"But the terms? Does your father demand an exorbitant amount of what we will take from the southerners?"

Siward leaned back and drained his horn of ale and beckoned a slave come refill it. He replied, "Oh, of course he did. He could not do otherwise. He is an intelligent man. Your people will doubtless be counting and handling the treasure we take. You will be sending his tribute along at whatever figure you deem believable. And my father has no way of knowing what you will actually earn. So he is obligated to name an outrageous figure so you do not completely chop him at the knees. He wants half of what we take."

Adalwolf laughed. "I assure you I intend no deception toward your father. That seems fair, you bring less men than I but more quality, perhaps. Then it is settled!"

Siward raised a hand. "Not quite. I am responsible for all of this, ultimately. And I require a payment."

"What do you want?"

Siward's cold blue eyes scanned the assembled.

"Her."

Adalwolf felt a sudden pit is his stomach. He spoke through clenched teeth. "Phaidyme."

"Yes, the foreign woman. She is still your slave, no?"

"Yes, but…"

Siward asked, "But what? Has she borne you children?"

"No."

"Then what is the problem? I think it is a more than fair trade. One slave for an army. Now that I speak it out loud it sounds ridiculous. But I must have her. I have never seen her like anywhere. I wonder if in her own country all the women look like that. That would be funny, would it not? And here we are, haggling over just one!"

Adalwolf's face had gone red. His knuckles were white as he clutched the spear. Othmar and Hartmut sensed his boiling rage. They leaned in.

Othmar laid a hand on his lord's shoulder. "Lord Adalwolf, what troubles you? Lord Siward could not have possibly offered insult," he spoke, seeking to allay trouble. Hartmut placed his hand on the sword at his hip.

Siward answered instead. "I asked a boon from your lord. A simple thing. But it troubles him. I understand. I was sentimental once." He patted Adalwolf's arm. "I had not anticipated your reluctance. Did you know the people of the south are known for their strong emotions in matters of the heart? Perhaps that is what draws you there."

Hartmut noticed the spear shook ever so slightly in his lord's grasp.

Siward continued. "Lord Adalwolf, let me apologize preemptively lest you think I offer insult. My comments were meant only to amuse, to illuminate. We have broken bread together and drank together. The men see we are friends. I may leave now without offering offense and retire to my camp. Give me your answer tonight. If you cannot part with the woman then I will march home in the morning, assuming I can maintain control of my host. I will tell my father you refused his terms. I will say you did so honorably lest our houses come to feuding. But you will be forced to march south without my men. You are a brave man but you know you don't have a chance without my spears. It will simply be a cattle raid. I bid you good evening, Lord Adalwolf."

He embraced his host and left.

Othmar and Hartmut spoke earnestly with their lord but he did not hear. He saw their mouths move, their gestures, but in his ears was only noise. He mumbled something about fresh air and left the hall. The two followed.

"My lord, what did he say?"

The warlord shook his head then peered upwards. Countless stars shined in a cloudless sky. A faint band of diffuse light marked the river of dead, snaking its way across the dark expanse. Athan breathed deep and closed his eyes. Throughout his life he felt he could sense his father watching him. In times of great danger he imagined he could almost hear the old man's voice travelling across the barrier between worlds. But now was only silence. After a last moment he gave up listening. He turned to Othmar.

"He said he will march with us. But he wants Phaidyme. He wants her as a gift."

Othmar spoke, "So what is the problem?"

Hartmut hissed, "What is the problem? She is his woman! They have shared a bed for many seasons. Have you no heart, sword-brother?"

"My lord, are you considering not granting his request? He will not march with us unless she is handed over, correct?"

"That is correct. And my heart is heavy. I do not want to

give her up."

Hartmut spat. "You should have married her."

"I would have, had the wounds Sigga caused ever healed. I could not trust her."

Othmar shook his head. "Well, no matter. My lord, you cannot chose the love of one woman over the chance for eternal glory. It is not simply loot we seek, as you taught us. We seek to change the world. Our people will be ruled by a great king as in other nations. The king will dispense justice. No more endless vendetta and bloodshed. Our people will live in peace and come to rule all. My lord, you will see when we march, you will see how they live in the south. They shape stone into images of men, women, gods. They live in halls of granite and marble with floors that are warm in the winter. I have seen it! And our people live in squalor! You will unmake the world and fashion it into something better! You, my lord, my king! You cannot abandon this vision for one woman, a slave at that!"

Adalwolf was motionless a moment, then slowly began to nod.

"You are right."

"Thank the gods, you see reason, lord. I shall have men take her to his camp."

Adalwolf only nodded. Hartmut shook his head. When his lord looked to him he averted his eyes. Othmar shouted for men from the hall and gave the orders as the three stood there under the night sky.

Phaidyme could see from the language of their bodies that they brought ill-tidings, the men that approached her in the hall. A wave of fear came and went as quick, replaced by the grim fatalism she had learned from her hosts. Othmar bade her follow him and made for the door of the hall. Ima looked with concern.

"What is happening? Why are you so grim, Othmar?"

Radobod stood, "Yes, brother, what business do you and this funeral party have with Phaidyme? Where is Lord Adalwolf? Is he fine?"

"Our lord is fine. The young woman must come with me. It is our lord's wish, the lord we swore an oath to serve. Now, go back to your drinking."

Radobod growled as he sat. Ima looked on as they left. A hand fell on her shoulder. There stood Kolkoi. His swarthy face was dark with worry.

He spoke, carefully picking his words in the speech of the tribes of hill and forest. "Where go daughter of the east?"

With some difficulty Ima explained what had just transpired. The other men of the steppe came to crowd around Kolkoi. His speech grew in volume as the group argued, strident gesticulations uncharacteristic for these dour men who spoke softly, voices like the sound of an arrow's flight. Ima thought the group would come to blows before the men finally bowed to the force of Kolkoi's will. They returned to the back of the hall. All but Kolkoi. With set expression he left the hall in haste.

The cool air washed over them like water from a fast brook after the heat of the hall.

"Othmar, what is happening?"

"You are to be given to Lord Siward."

The woman stopped in her tracks.

Othmar turned. "Come, Phaidyme. It was the man's price for joining the host. None want this but it simply must happen. Now, you can walk or be carried, it matters not to me."

Though her heart's worst fears were realized, Phaidyme made no trouble. She had cried all the tears she would ever cry when first taken from her home. This betrayal was simply another chapter. To the gods she whispered curses, a curse for giving her beauty, a curse for sending her north, a curse for the gift of her heart, inclined to love and to trust. She cursed Adalwolf and prayed for his demise. The heat of anger worked upon her heart, a forge to make armor against sadness.

Siward's host was camped in the fields outside the village. Simple tents of rough wool were laid out haphazardly, the scene illuminated by scores of bonfires around which sat men drinking and talking.

Siward called to Othmar, jogging toward him with some of his bodyguard in tow. The firelight showed the joy on his face as he recognized Phaidyme.

Othmar raised his hand in greeting as the two parties met.

"Here is my lord's gift, Lord Siward."

"Excellent! We will indeed march tomorrow. Come here, young woman, let me look upon you."

He reached forward to push aside the hood of her cloak. She recoiled. Othmar grabbed her arm and pushed her forward.

Othmar let loose a sudden cry of pain.

The torch's light showed an arrow's head which had emerged from just beneath his sternum. He regarded it a moment before crumpling to the ground, face fixed with an expression of utter incomprehension.

Men drew weapons and unslung their shields. Cries of "Ambush!" and "Murder!" rang out in the night.

From the gloom came a shout, voice deep and tongue

strange. Phaidyme bolted toward the sound. Siward caught her arm and pulled her back. She swung about and raked her nails across his face, opening deep gouges. He lost his grip and screamed in rage.

There was the sound of hooves beating the packed earth and suddenly Phaidyme stood before Kolkoi, reaching down from atop his rearing mount.

From the dimness came the airy whistle of something moving at speed. Phaidyme watched as Kolkoi fell from the saddle with a groan, landing on his back. His dark face was deeply furrowed as he pulled Siward's axe from his sternum. Phaidyme was beside him.

Though it clearly pained him deeply, he spoke again, one word in the harsh tongue of his home. "Run!"

Phaidyme fled, aided by the darkness, a prayer for Kolkoi on her lips, a prayer to a sky god that she knew not. He was their god, the god of the steppe, the god of soaring hawks and running horses. He was perhaps even crueler than the gods of the north, a god that suffered no weakness amongst those that lived in his wide domain. But Phaidyme prayed that Kolkoi's soul would be given a reward. A horse that needed no watering, a bow that never broke, a horizon which would swallow no sun, so that he may ride and hunt forever in plains caressed by gentle wind.

So she thought as she fled for her life.

Siward turned to his men. "Fetch torches! You will hunt down this hare and bring her to me! Return with her or do not return! Go!"

The men of the steppe took the corpse of their leader. They wept openly, an act not shameful amidst their people. They rode away in darkness, heading east, never to be seen again.

Gasto was woken by the whispering of a bat. He leapt from his bed of grass and took in the air. A gentle breeze brought scents from the west. There was steel and burning pitch. There was another scent, familiar, but sour with fear.

He ran, scrambling over fallen trees and ducking under branches. His chest burned but he dare not slow. Ahead her form cut a silhouette against the white columns of birch that glowed so faintly in the moon's light.

"Phaidyme! What is happening?"

She reeled at the sound of his voice but recovered quickly.

"Gasto! Your brother betrayed me. Siward's men pursue me. My doom comes, as foreseen."

The shaman grabbed her hand and the two ran. Ahead to the right Gasto spied the bobbing light of a torch. He altered course, only to see more lights to his left.

"They have flanked us! We have to beat them to the stream ahead. There is only one place nearby where it may be forded."

They pushed on. Above the moon rose to its zenith, bright enough to cast shadows underneath. Phaidyme's legs ached as her face and arms were attacked by brush. Gasto heard the thunder of blood pumping in his ears. Ahead a low rise beckoned, the stream was on the other side. He made a noise of triumph, premature.

Two men on horseback waited below.

Gasto cursed. He pulled Phaidyme back but Siward's men had gained. The bobbing lights now illuminated the faces of warriors exultant in the chase, their quarry sighted.

They called to each other, cornering their prey. Phaidyme and Gasto stood with their back to the rise, nowhere left to go.

"They only want me. Slip away, Gasto, go!" She pushed

him but he shook his head.

"Very noble, sister, but too late."

Ten men advanced, weapons drawn. They were leisurely in their manner, catching their breath from the pursuit, savoring their success. Behind the pair the two men on horse stood atop the rise.

Their leader was a tall man painted for war, black bands crossing his face and bare chest. He bore a shield and hunting spear and wore a fine sword at his waist.

His bearded face grinned. "Come, girl, the game is over. You should thank the gods you belong to my lord lest I be the one to punish you for bolting. Come nicely and I will let you ride a horse back to your master."

"Who is this other one?", asked a warrior.

"I do not know. But it is good he is here. His death will slake my anger at being sent on such an errand as this."

Phaidyme was silent. Her mind raced but could find no answer, no way out.

Gasto leaned down, whispering in her ear.

"Close your eyes."

"What?"

"You should not see this."

The horses screamed first, throwing their riders as the clearing was suddenly alive with bounding gray shapes. Their fur shone silver in the moon's light, eyes black and fangs yellow tinged gray.

The wolves attacked each man in twos and threes. The erstwhile hunters could not even bring weapons to bear in the suddenness of the assault. The forest became a theater for a drama as old as life, scenes of primordial violence, the red poetry of predator upon prey. Cracked bone and torn jugular, severed tendon and sundered flesh, living things become food for other living things. Victims disarmed, flesh rent and brought low, the wolves began to feast while yet their victims still breathed, starting always where the prey was softest, the belly. The screams echoed from the trunks, a chorus of agony floating upwards on the cool air. In the moonlight the blood was black, streaking the trunks as the terrible feast reached its fever pitch.

"We must move away, but slowly. I know them, and they know me, but they are crazed now, mad with the feast, all the more so as they savor the flesh of men, a rare treat."

The pair made their way from the clearing slowly.

Gasto sighed in relief as they reached the streams edge.

He spoke, exhaustion weighing his words. "I think I saw the horses bolt north. We shall find them."

"And then where will we go?"

The shaman shrugged. "Anywhere."


Adalwolf passed a restless night. What sleep he had was spoiled by dreams. In the night visions he saw a procession of all the people lost to him, some dead, others by circumstance. His father and mother and sisters passed by, refusing to meet his gaze. There was Thankarat, body rent with wounds, and Gasto, holding court as he sat on a tree stump, attended by wolves. There was Othmar on his funeral pyre and Kolkoi's body, held aloft by his kinsmen, taken to be buried in secret as was their way. Finally Phaidyme, face betraying no emotion, looking at him as one would a stranger.

He rose with the dawn and summoned his bodyguard and the warlords which now served him.

The group numbered over a hundred as each warlord brought a few of his own guard. Sigils and banners were held aloft on poles. Some bore a picture, like Adalwolf's wolf. Others were idols, crude depictions of the War God or All-Father, some of his wife, a goddess of planting and wisdom. Some were decorated with heads tied to cross poles by their hair, others bore the skull of auroch or wolf. When the group had assembled in the field Adalwolf and his guard walked in procession, coming to stand before them. Siward was clearly out of sorts. Adalwolf regarded the scratches on his face with fresh pangs of guilt, having reached the most logical interpretation. The northern lord noticed his attention but made no comment.

Hartmut produced a cloth bag, drawing from it a crown of gold, fashioned without skill and set with one ruby in the center. The stone was held in place by two wolves. The crown was passed to each warlord in turn. When all had touched the article Siward placed it upon Adalwolf's head. Two young men led a white stallion to the clearing. The proud beast shook his head and snorted as it neared Adalwolf.

Hartmut stroked its face but the horse would not calm. "Pity those that seem to know what is coming."

Two more of the guard, Radobod and Odalric, Hartmut's brother, moved to grab the stallion's rope collar. Adalwolf drew his saex and turned to Hartmut.

"Save your pity. Before the moon is full again many of us will die by blade or arrow. A prick and then he bleeds out in but a moment. We should be so lucky."

The stallion kicked as Radobod and Odalric tightened their grasp. Adalwolf aimed the dagger at the beast's neck and thrust. At that moment the horse pitched itself forward. What had meant to be a stab into the jugular was spoiled. The blade's sharp point found the jugular but then was pulled downward, opening a rough gash from which poured forth blood, hot and thick. The stallion reared, throwing the two men backwards as it screamed.

Adalwolf ducked its kicking forelegs as the blood sprayed, covering his face and darkening the fine furs draped around his shoulders. The warlord reeled, stumbling backwards, cursing. The horse kicked and jumped, tossing its head back and forth as it spun in awkward circles, Adalwolf underfoot. He thrust up with the spear, impaling the poor creature.

To watch a horse running through a meadow is to know a purpose fulfilled, to witness a sort of nobility only present in nature. In its death throes the stallion was the antithesis. The rhythm of its gait, the grace of its long limbs, gone, replaced by pitiable awkwardness as it screamed, eyes mad with fear and pain. The stallion reared one last time and collapsed, half on Adalwolf.

His guard ran to his side, pushing the carcass away and pulling him to his feet. Odalric was pale, worry writ across his ruddy face.

"The gods, they reject the sacrifice…"

Adalwolf snarled, grabbing the man and pushing him down. He cast his eyes over the assembled and shouted, "The gods will accept what I give them! The sacrifice is complete!"

The warlords began the chant, taken up by the whole host.

"King Adalwolf!"

Horns blew and spears were beat against shields as they marched south.

Three day's walk took them to the banks of the river which separated north and south. The host marched to where the river was spanned by a wooden bridge of southern construction, wide enough to accommodate a cart led by oxen and still have room for others to pass alongside.

On the far bank a fortress of stout timber stood watch over the bridge. Most of the men had never seen a structure so large. The fear grew as those with experience warned their sword-brothers of the shower of missiles that would rain down upon the men when they neared its thick wooden walls.

"Where are their soldiers?"

Radobod shook his head. "I know not, king. They must hide behind the walls, waiting our approach. Their chieftains are clever men. Perhaps they do so to hide their numbers before the arrows come."

Adalwolf stepped onto the bridge first. He walked with spear and shield raised. The anticipation of bloody battle lent speed to his steps. He broke into a jog, raising his shield above him, waiting for the sound of arrows striking the ash. The host's steps made a thunderous noise on the planks underfoot.

But no missiles came.

The warriors rammed down the doors of the towers and stole inside, only to emerge moments later to report them empty.

Radobod shook his head. "It is not a good sign, my king. They knew of our approach. It is to be expected, I suppose. Word of your army must have spread far and wide."

Hartmut contradicted his sword-brother. "The men who live in the towers simply fled. Their courage failed at the sight of us. I am not afraid."

Radobod growled in reply, "Nor am I! I only worry they may have gathered a host to rival ours had they enough warning."

Adalwolf regarded the spear in his hands. He smiled as he spoke, "It matters not either way. All will fall before our blades. The Black Oaks will drown in southern blood."

The men sent up a cheer. Radobod joined his voice with theirs even as his eyes scanned the far hills.

The settlement was deserted. No soldier nor merchant nor farmer walked its wide lanes or hid within its houses of stone and timber.

The host continued south. A storm grew above. Gray clouds rode on the back of a galloping wind from the south. The clouds blotted out the sun but no rain came.

Scouts knelt before Adalwolf and gave a breathless report of the enemy massed in great numbers ahead.

The host reached the crest of the hill and Adalwolf saw them.

On the meadow below they waited, arrayed in great blocks, one after another, thousands upon thousands. Each block of men boasted its own sigil and horns. Chieftains walked amidst the ranks, resplendent in helms of gleaming bronze and tall crests of stiff horse hair. Thousands of men standing still, awaiting the order from their leaders, representatives of the far away god king of the south who dwelt in halls of marble and hanging silk. The heads of their spears shimmered, a grassland of sharp steel.

The southerners had known. They had learned of Adalwolf's march and were prepared.

Adalwolf felt his heart swell. The southerners had so many. But he had the spear. He would kill hundreds himself. They would overcome. What now belonged to these arrogant men would become his.

His host formed a line. A great roar rose up from the men as each gave voice to his hatred for the soldiers below.

Above swirled clouds of thick gray.

Hartmut shouted above the din. "What in the names of all

the gods is that old man doing?"

Adalwolf followed his gaze to the center of the meadow. There walked a tall man, gray beard spilling from underneath his gray hood. None of the southerners seemed to take notice. On long strides the old man walked up the gentle slope, making for the center where stood Adalwolf and his guard.

Many had noticed and had given up their war cries to murmur amidst themselves. The old man walked with purpose. As he neared Adalwolf felt heavier, as if the earth's power had grown, pulling him down. All now watched, silent, words smothered in their throats. Adalwolf peered at the old man, unable to see his eyes from under the hood. Finally the man came to stand before him. Hartmut stared, mouth open.

The warlord could find no words as the old man met his gaze. A gray cloth covered his left eye. The other was colored the blue of glaciers and pierced Adalwolf to his bones, an icy steel thrust deep. The two stood, eyes locked.

The old man took the spear. Adalwolf thought to resist but there was no strength in his limbs. What had been given was taken away.

The old man took a step backward and then all was awash in blinding light as thunder boomed across the meadow, echoing from the hills.

When Adalwolf opened his eyes the old man was gone. He stood dumb.

Hartmut spoke, barely above a whisper, "The spear. I had wondered. The All-Father has removed his favor. You have displeased him..."

Adalwolf glared from underneath his helmet. Hartmut shook his head. His king grabbed his collar and pulled him close.

"Damn the All-Father! Where was he when my father's

hall burned? Where was he when Thankarat was slain? Where was he when Sigmar made his demand and took her…"

For a moment he could not continue. He spat on the ground at Hartmut's feet.

"I need no favor! I need no spear! I have many thousands of men! My arm and blade! I curse all else! Do you hear me?"

Adalwolf stepped forward and turned to his men who looked on. They were yet in shock from the apparition that had taken the spear, though most could not even tell what had transpired. But none had mistook it for a good omen.

Adalwolf's voice rang out, rough with hate as he spoke, "Curse them all! Curse the southerners! Curse the weak and the cowardly! Curse the very gods who watch now! Curse them!" Tears of rage streaked down his handsome face, now a demon's mask. "All will fall before us! We are born to a world of death and injustice! So let us become death! Let our blades speak the truth of our lives! We are death! Death!" His words fell away, footprints washed away by lapping waves. He howled into the wind as he drew his sword. His madness spread like fire fed from summer's warm wind. His men howled with him, relishing a truth none thought to ever speak.

Whistles sounded across the meadow. With impossible precision the southerners began to march forward.

The King of the Black Oaks, of Hills and Forests, raised his sword as he howled. He felt the strength of his limbs, the heavy blade light in his hand, his armor light on his back. The battle madness came. He was given over to death, the warrior's paradox; the best chance to survive is to no longer care. He cared not whether he was victorious. He cared for nothing. There was only the howl burning his throat, his blade and the foes which approached on deliberate steps even as Adalwolf and his men broke into a run. A peculiar kind of impatience lent force to their steps, black souls hungry for blood and death even if it be their own.

The southern chieftains barked orders in their staccato tongue and the sky became black with arrows. From the ranks of Adalwolf's host a chorus of screams arose. The men broke into a sprint, desperate to close with their enemies. Closer they came and the southerners let loose their heavy javelins. Men fell to Adalwolf's right and left. He knocked one of the missiles aside with his shield and found he could now meet their eyes. Underneath helmets of bronze their faces were a catalog of emotion, some fearful, others determined, swarthy jaw set grim. But their discipline held as the mass of warriors thundered down upon their lines.

On a low rise behind the blocks of men stood the southern warlords astride mounts of dappled gray or white. Gold decorated the elaborate helmets over sharp faced features, all beardless. Purple capes fluttered in the gentle breeze. Adalwolf fixed his eyes on him that must have been the chieftain, the warlord of warlords, a middle aged man who sat on his mount with arms folded, surrounded by attendants. The man's face betrayed no emotion. The cavalrymen at his flanks stood like statues, silver masks obscuring their features.

Adalwolf saw him not as a man but as prey. He craved his blood as a wolf craves deer. He lowered his eyes to the foes directly ahead, the line of shields held steady against the mad charge. His howl still tore his throat as the two forces met with a deafening crash.

Suddenly those in front were now close as lovers, stabbing and hacking even as their sword brothers pushed from behind, a mass of steel and flesh pushing forward. The ground was churned under their feet as they fought. The southerners held their shields tight, working their short blades from behind its safety, parrying, thrusting, while the second rank lashed out when an enemy came in range. Adalwolf bashed down again and again, towering over his foes. The speed and savagery of his strikes was such to give the soldiers no chance to swing back. His blade split a helmet then struck again, finding the neck of one on his right. He tasted the man's blood as it spurt from the open jugular. He pushed forward in the gap and struck again. His soul filled with elation. They had penetrated the line. They had only to keep pushing.

A whistle sounded and the men to his front melted away, never dropping their guard. Adalwolf screamed in triumph, sound dying in his throat as another block jogged into place before him. The host hammered into the fresh line, though this time with less strength. Adalwolf felled the man in front of him and spared a glance upward. The southern chieftain stood as before, calm. With a wave of his hand the cavalry sped off to the left. The savage king felt a blow glance off his helmet and returned to the fray with a growl, sending his blade into his assailant's gut.

A fresh chorus of screams from his left erupted as the horses struck the flank where Adalwolf's men had made little impact on the line. He looked to the right and realized that there also the charge had failed. Adalwolf and his guard had pierced deep but now their flanks were exposed. A horn blew and was answered by whistles and the blocks shifted, pushing forward to further isolate Adalwolf and his chosen men.

A javelin from the side pierced his shoulder. He cursed and tore the long point away then stumbled. An explosion of blue stars clouded his vision as another blow struck his helm. He stood and swung his blade in a mighty arc that took the man's head from his shoulders.

He saw Hartmut fall beside him, blood streaming from his torn throat. Radobod was next, a blade pushed through his mail and deep into his heart. Adalwolf bashed the man with his shield, taking him off his feet. He buried his sword in the man's face before one of their heavy blades sank deep into his shoulder. His arm went limp and his shield fell to the ground.

He was surrounded. Blades found his arms, his legs, his chest. He felt the strength ebb from his body but still he fought, howling and howling, a wounded wolf, teeth bared and eyes glossy with desperate hate. He raised his arm to strike yet again but a spear pierced his side and he reeled. Another, then another and another sank deep as he fell to his knees. He died with arm still raised, eyes toward the gray sky where two ravens circled, watching his doom.

The End